THE TRAIN ROBBERS

THE TRAIN ROBBERS

JOHN DYSON

A Black Horse Western

ROBERT HALE · LONDON

ISBN 0 7090 4864 5

Robert Hale Limited
Clerkenwell House
Clerkenwell Green
London EC1R 0HT

Photoset in North Wales by
Derek Doyle & Associates, Mold, Clwyd.
Printed in Great Britain by
St Edmundsbury Press Ltd, Bury St Edmunds, Suffolk.
Bound by WBC Bookbinders Ltd, Bridgend, Mid-Glamorgan.

ONE

There was a festive air about the occasion: flags and bunting decorating the small railroad terminus of Red Rock. A crowd had gathered in their best bib and tucker, ladies in long summer muslin, storekeepers and farmers in hot Sunday suits sporting silk plug hats, derbys and bold gold watch chains. They were all waiting to ride on the new railroad headed south across Indian Territory towards the Texas state line.

Missouri, Kansas, and Texas Railway, a notice tacked to the clapboard wall hopefully stated. *75 miles of staging saved: 36 hours quicker than by any other route! The El Paso stage company makes close connection at the end of the track.*

A tall lean man stood in the shade of the booking hall canopy, dark brooding eyes beneath his wide-brimmed hat, watching the activity as folk milled about. He struck a match on his high-heeled riding boot and put the flame to a ten cent cigar.

'Ain't thet jest dandy?' he drawled to an Indian youth who squatted by his side. 'They got an iron track headin' toward Texas now. One of these days they'll be able to roll their cows the whole durn way in wagons. Sure will beat three months on the trail.'

The Indian, a Wichita, was rigged up partly cowpuncher style, and partly native. He was slim in a

5

dusty black velvet shirt over cotton pants, secured by a leather belt, into which were stuck a long-barrelled revolver and a vicious hunting knife. He had tasselled soft boots on his feet, and a red headband binding his long black hair beneath a high-topped Stetson. There was a necklace of beads at his throat.

'That'll be the day,' he said.

The older man, Pete Bowen, spat a gob of brown juice from the cheap cigar that had partly disintegrated in his mouth. He flicked it away with disgust into the dust. 'They look a mighty prosperous bunch of folks.'

'I wanna git me a watch and chain like that,' the Wichita grunted, his eyes on a wiry little man in a conductor's hat and ill-fitting suit who was studying a big gold watch on his spread palm.

'Any minute she'll be arriving, folks,' the little man yelled. 'Have you all got your tickets? Don't fergit, our fares are as low as any other competing line.'

The township, a collection of stores and saloons and grain silos, stood beneath its eponymous red rock, humped egg-like over it, a landmark on the plain. It was farming country. These people, once rough and ready settlers, had been made prosperous through the discovery by Memmonite farmers of how wheat could be properly cultivated under the blazing sun in these parts. Most of them would be going for the ride and the social occasion and coming back again.

Not many would be venturing further than the 75 miles to Connor's Crossing because once the river was passed you were venturing into strange domains where Indians roamed.

Pete and his Wichita friend watched with interest as a light surrey came wheeling in along the dusty main street, its high-stepping strutter pulled in to a halt by a debonair sandy-haired man at the reins. By his side was a haughty young woman dressed in green silk candy stripe, a little pill box hat and veil perched on her Irish-red braids.

'You sure cuttin' it fine, Mistuh Baxter,' the wiry official in the conductor's hat shouted out. 'Is Katherine going all the way?'

'She sure is,' Baxter said. 'She's going to spend a few weeks with that no-good fiancé of hers, see how he's getting on with building the bridge.'

Most of the people laughed, for they wished to keep in with Mr Baxter, and far from being no-good (in their eyes) his daughter Katherine's betrothed was a real go-getter and prosperous man. The US government was putting big bucks into backing the railway companies, the aim being to spread civilization into the wilderness. John Chiltern was superintending building the new line and was buying up land where need be.

The official helped the young lady to step down. She was dressed in the height of fashion. 'She's got one of them newfangled arse coolers,' a lady muttered, noting the bustle bulging out the back of her skirts.

Pete shook his head with incomprehension. A mighty funny get-up to be setting out on a journey into Indian country. How the hell was she planning to sit down in the train with that thing on her backside and her waist wasped in tight with lace stays no doubt?

'Ain't ya sceered goin' all that way on your own, Miss Katherine?' the lady asked in a reedy voice. 'And without a chaperone?'

Another added, disapprovingly, 'Modern girls!'

'Daddy wanted to come with me, but I wouldn't think of it. He's got his business to attend to. I can look after myself. I'm a Baxter, you know.'

Her smile froze as she spotted the official struggling to get her trunk from the back of the buckboard, tipping it onto its side. 'Oh, do be careful, Mr Mirick. Really! Can't you manage?'

She swivelled her neck and her green eyes met the dark ones of the broad chested stranger standing in the shade. He looked like a down-at-heel cowpuncher returning home from a cattle drive or he might not have been.

'I say, you there. Could you possibly?'

Pete paused for a few seconds, a smile flickering on his lips, holding her regard, and languidly pushed himself away with his elbows from the wall, and, with a gloved hand, swung the trunk onto his shoulder. He carried it, with a long stride, and dumped it upside down by the iron rails.

'Oh, my God,' she scolded. 'Men!'

Pete rolled it upright with his boot. 'Guess you must've got bottles of French parfoom in that? Sure hope they ain't leaked.'

'Here,' she said, opening her little fringed bag and thrusting a silver dollar at him. 'Leave it there.'

He grinned, widely, taking the dollar, as if with awe, in two fingers, poking it into the pocket of his red wool shirt, and touching the fingers to his hat. 'Thank you kindly, miss.'

He went to unhitch his black stallion and grey mare because the clang of a swinging bell, the huff-huff-huff of a smoke stack, and the whoo-whoo of a steam whistle had announced the approach of the sturdy little 'Katie' engine and its two passenger cars and freight vans that had come all the way from Kansas City.

The Wichita youth, who was known by his tribe as Howling Wolf, but preferred to be known by his 'civilized' name of Henry Littlejohn, padded after him and untied the pack mule and his Appaloosa pony.

'The young white lady very generous and gracious to

you, huh?' His impassive copper-bronze features lit up with a smile. 'Maybe she like to give you more than just a dollar?'

His morose companion, who he had been riding with for two months past, nodded, and shortened his stirrup. 'Mebbe.'

The locomotive had hissed and wheezed and grunted into the once terminus, from hereon merely to become a passing halt, roaring and billowing clouds of smoke and steam, passengers yelling and jumping out, others loading their baggage on, while the engine took on wood and water. Black Pete and the Indian loaded their horses onto an open car.

'Enjoy the ride, hoss,' Pete said, fondling the mare's ears. He had had her twelve years but had never got round to giving her a handle. He gave the stallion a friendly punch on the jaw and jumped down.

In front of the locomotive a little ceremony was in process. Mr Mirick who, it seemed, was the general freight and ticket agent was giving a speech to the effect that only a year before, the railroad had crossed the Arkansas for the first time and here they were. And before long they'd be moving a network into Texas, who knew, even to San Antone itself, and that was progress. 'Yassuh!'

And he was handing a large pair of scissors to Miss Katherine Baxter, who snipped through a blue ribbon across the pristine track, and they all huzzaed and tossed their hats in the air, and one or two were firing off revolvers. The bell was clanging and they hurried to jump aboard and find their places and wave out of the windows as the train clattered and groaned as the loco built up steam – chuf-chuf-chuf whoooooohoooooo! – and they went rolling away out of the Red Rock. Soon the fenced-in farms were all passed and they were out in the wide open spaces.

TWO

Howling Wolf, or Henry Littlejohn, watched the white people making merry, contempt flickering in his slits of eyes as he sat straight-backed beside his friend as the carriages rocked and swayed. Hampers had been opened, chicken drumsticks, hogpie and cherry cake were being stuffed greedily into mouths. Stone flagons of liquor and beer were being passed around among the ham-fisted farmers sweating in their hairy broadcloth suits. Some had got loudly vociferous, boasting of the sharp deals they had made, others singing, trying to egg the others on to join in. Occasionally some would give wild whoops as they spotted a buffalo herd by the side of the rails, grabbing their six-shooters, hanging from the windows and blazing away to bring the sullen dark beasts down, leaving them to rot by the side of the rails. Then they crowed about how many they had got. In ten years the vast herds had been decimated. And they called the Indians savages.

Since the eighteenth century a Wichita Indian village had prospered near Red Rock, south-west of the Arkansas River. His people had traded with the Spanish and French and later with the Americans on the cattle trails and stage routes. They had been guaranteed by Washington a perpetual home in Indian Territory.

Prior to the Civil War the Indians had had their own farms, had traded black slaves, buffalo robes, lariats, rawhide and blankets. Now that was all gone.

The Wichita Indians had suffered badly for supporting the south. After the war the northerners had punished them by confiscating their lands, freeing their slaves, moving them away, halving Indian Territory. Howling Wolf had been taken from his family as a boy, and, as part of a 'progressive' government experiment, sent away to the north-east to a white college to be educated in white men's ways. He had known little of what was going on 'back home' until, in the lawless years after the war at the age of seventeen, he had returned.

There had been no 'home' to return to. The white settlers had moved in to live under the Indians' sacred hill of Red Rock, had fenced off their lands. His parents had died of smallpox. His grandmother and sister had been tolerated to live on a patch of scrubby land that nobody wanted where they eked a living.

Howling Wolf, or Henry Littlejohn, had taken to wandering, drinking, robbing, sometimes working, moving on. It was as if he was caught in a no man's land, between two cultures. He had little in common with the men of his own tribe, or with the white men. Indian-baiting was common fun in small settlements, and in one of them, Gallows Crossing in Colorado, he had come off the worse. He was being kicked around in the dust when this man, Black Pete, had stepped in, and his fists swinging, had given his tormentors a whupping.

Since then they had ridden together and Pete had talked about heading farther out West, staking a piece of ground, and getting some new roots.

He, too, had been living on the edge, a one-time Deputy Marshal, who had turned outlaw, always moving on, hounded by his own people. Pete's idea had appealed to Howling Wolf, but only if he could take his family: his grandmother and sister.

'Why not?' Pete had shrugged. 'Somebody gotta do the weavin' an' cookin'. The more the merrier.'

So, they had drifted back to Red Rock. Two days ago that would have been. There had been an uneasy atmosphere in the saloon when they had tethered their tired horses and walked in. Men huddled, casting glances at Pete's well-used Smith and Wesson revolvers, handles forward, on his hips, the rifle tucked under his arm.

Something, apparently, had been going on two nights before. Some of Mr Baxter's bully boys had come into town, shooting their mouths and their guns off. Howling Wolf noticed a newspaper on the saloon counter and his blood froze as he read the editorial, a series of simple paragraphs, one of which casually remarked, 'Some of the boys must have had themselves a good time Tuesday night by the sound of the gunshots. In the morning a squaw was found hung up on the flagpole.'

He had arrived two days too late. The squaw was his sister. Their grandmother had died a month before. He had no family. His tribe moved to other lands. Howling Wolf watched the fat white men, most of them from Red Rock, cavorting. He wondered if any of the young oafs shooting the buffalo had raped and murdered his sister. Did it matter? He wanted vengeance. On all of them.

Black Pete opened his eyes, pushed his long hair from his forehead and awoke from his catnap. The sound of the engine had changed, become more pushing, more laboured. Clouds of smoke rolled past the windows. The telegraph wire rose and fell, hypnotically. They were climbing up into hill country, careering around sheer gorges, passing through tunnels blasted out of the rock, rattling over high trestle bridges.

He experienced a sense of emptiness as he looked down at the chasm, a thin silver stream rushing far below, as he thought of what he had to do. He had had a run of bad luck, the cards hadn't fallen right. Somehow his dollars had been frittered away since leaving Colorado. He needed another grubstake if he were to go further West. Maybe they should have taken the bank in Red Rock?

He felt sorry about what had happened to Howling Wolf's sister, and kinda guilty because it had been done by white men. The Indian was a good kid. But, what could you do? What chance was there of finding the men or boys responsible? As soon as he and Howling had arrived in town a resentful wall of silence had been put up. The editor of the newspaper claimed not to know. The Red Rock sheriff didn't want to know either. He had warned them to get out of town. Maybe that was the best idea or they, too, would have ended hanging from the flagpole. Nobody in that town gave a damn about some young squaw the boys had had their fun with. Damn redlegs and farmers, damn bluebelly Yankees. Once he had put his life on the line, in places like Abilene and Dodge City, to defend people like these. Now it was different. He sensed an edge of excitement fluttering through him. He had no qualms about what he was going to do.

Pete nudged Howling Wolf and they casually stood and stretched, as if they were going out to stand on the viewing platform to smoke cigars.

'What a hullabaloo in there,' Pete said, as he closed the door, and they stood rocking from side to side, watching blue silhouettes of mountains go by. The sun was going down and the sky was ravaged red as if the prairies were on fire. 'I reckon we better make our move.'

Howling Wolf leapt onto the first flatcar and, in moccasin boots, moved swiftly over the cargo of pig iron. Pete followed, more awkward in his riding boots, the ground flying past beneath him, as he jumped for the second wagon. 'I'm gittin' too old fer this job,' he growled, as Howling pulled him aboard, and took a sawn-off shotgun from the pack of his horse. Pete patted the mare and stallion and headed for the caboose.

He pulled his thick red bandanna up over his face – although people had already seen him it kinda let them know what he was about – and took his right hand .44 out, and smashed the glass of the final wagon, thrusting the revolver through the bars.

'All right, Mr Mirick, open this door if you wanna stay alive,' he shouted. 'Don't play the hero.'

Mirick had been caught unawares sat in his armchair. He put his hands up and his frightened face appeared. 'What'n hell you boys want?'

Pete caught him by the collar. 'That safe open. Or else. Me and my Injin pal ain't feelin' too friendly towards the people of Red Rock.'

'Ain't nuthin' in thar, ahm tellin' ya. You're wasting your time.'

'Do you want me to smash your skull in and take the keys for myself.'

'No ... no need to be like that. You bought your ticket, after all.'

'Sure did,' Pete breathed, as the little guard let him in, rattled his keys and the safe door swung open. He hauled out a bag of silver dollars.

'How much in here?'

'Only a hundred. Told ya 'tweren't much.'

'You're holdin' out' – Pete thrust the barrel of his revolver into his throat – 'where's the rest?'

'There ain't none. The cupboard is bare, I swear. Why would we be taking cash to Connor's Crossing? There ain't nuthin' down there. Jest a load of scrub, a coupla tradin' stores and a construction gang building the bridge. They get paid when it's all done.'

'Shee-it!' Pete handed the bag to the Indian. 'Silver dollars. Hang it on your hoss. Looks like we're out of luck.'

'I'll make him talk,' Howling Wolf pulled his long scalping knife from its beaded scabbard, 'you watch.'

'It's the truth', the guard screamed, backing away.

'Aw, c'mon!' Pete hung onto Howling Wolf, worried he might be really thirsty for blood. 'There ain't nowhere else it can be. Mebbe we better see if these other buckaroos got a dime or two.'

They clambered back to the carriages and the Indian climbed to the roof and ran lightly along, leaping to the front one, swaying from side to side, smoke and sparks in his face as the locomotive chugged rythmically on.

Pete walked through the second carriage and reached the first one as the Indian appeared at the far end, the double barrels of Howling's shotgun looking ominous as he shouted, 'Hold it! Freeze!'

Women screamed, sleeping and startled men jumped to their feet, three going for their guns. The slug of Pete's .44 caught one in the shoulder, spinning him round. A youth turned to face him, a carbine in his hands. Pete shot his hat off and he dropped the weapon, scalded with fright. A bearded, burly storekeeper was still cursing and struggling to pull his six-gun from its holster when Howling Wolf's first barrel splattered its shot bloodily into his chest at close range.

The compartment reverberated with the explosions, gunsmoke drifting, as Pete hollered, 'Anybody else wan' it, they sure goin' git it. All you men, throw your guns down.'

Reluctantly, the weapons clattered to the floor – 'All of 'em, I said' – and a Bowie knife followed suit.

'Now ahm steppin' along among you with my gunny sack and yawl throw ya valuables in, you hear, wallets, jewellery, the lot. One dead's enough. We don't want no more. Ain't no point in resistin'.'

Everybody had gone quiet, making mental notes of how they could manage to hide a ring, or a wad of notes.

'Come along, suh. Thet ain't no good to us, nohow.' Pete recognized a scrawny-faced storekeeper from Red Rock. 'You tellin' me thet's all you got? Take your boot off. Let's see. Yeah, I mighta guessed. Toss it in the bag. We don't like cheats. And I remember you cheatin' me.'

Two scruffy unshaven cowpunchers were in one of the seats and scowled as they dug in their pockets.

'Where you boys goin'?'

'Back home to Texas.'

'Thet's okay. You can hang onto yourn.'

Howling Wolf threw all the guns he could find out of the windows of the rattling train and they went back to the other carriage, again attacking from both ends. This time there was no gunplay, the men cursing and whining, throwing down their gunbelts as the carriage rocked along.

'Do I gather from that badge on your hat you were with the blessed Confederacy?' an old gent with a white goatee and curled moustaches piped up. 'Are you still fighting the war?'

'You could say that, Grandad.' Pete recognized the Savannah drawl and passed him by, poking his revolver into the over-upholstered gut of an old biddy from Red Rock. 'Make it snappy, ma'am. Where've you got your money, in your drawers? We'll have that ring, too.'

'It won't come off,' she cried.

'Maybe I should cut it off,' the Indian said, and wrenched the gold and diamonds from her.

'Haven't any of you men any guts?' he heard a young voice ask. 'What are you, chicken-livered?'

'Why, Miss Baxter! I wonder what you've got in that portmanteau of yourn? Durn heavy enough fer gold.'

'You filthy prairie rat. How dare you come in here threatening ladies? Confederacy? You're nothing but rebels, thieves and murderers, bullies and cowards.'

'We all got a living to make. You got a key to thet thung? Or do I have to blow the lock off?'

The young woman drew herself up to her full height, looking down her long classical nose at him, her glassy green eyes fanatic and fiery. 'You touch one morsel of my property and my father will hunt you down. And so will my fiancé. There will be nowhere you can hide.'

'Thet so?' Pete pulled the trigger and the lock of the young lady's trunk was shattered. He dipped his hand in, pulling out dresses, negligees, stockings, corsets, and finally, necklaces and earrings, opals and amethysts. He stuffed the latter in his pocket and picked out a wallet. 'Ah, cash. Thet's more like it.'

Katherine's hand flashed out and caught him across the cheek, again and again, until he could grab her wrist, restrain her and with a push to her green silk-covered chest, replace her with a thump on her seat. 'Oh!' She gave a piercing indignant scream. 'He hit me. You saw that. This fine southern gentleman.'

'Shut up, you silly woman.' Pete's ear was stinging. 'Or maybe my friend will make you.'

He turned to Howling Wolf. 'Howdja like a fine red scalp on your lodge pole.'

Howling had never taken a scalp before. Nor lived in a teepee for a long time. But now he had killed his first man and he smiled, evilly, and drew his knife.

'He wouldn't,' the girl said.

'His sister was raped and murdered in thet so-called Christian town of yourn, so I wouldn't be too sure.'

The blood drained from her face as she stared at him so haughtily. 'His sister? That was nothing to do with us, the Baxters.'

'It was some of your boys. Would you blame him for wanting revenge?'

She fell silent, so he turned to the town mayor, corpulent in a frock coat and cravat. Pete took a diamond pin from his stock, and yanked the gold watch and chain from across his belly, dropping them into the bag. 'If your sheriff had done his duty mebbe me and my friend wouldn't be doin' this, Mr Mayor. Sorry to disturb your little excursion.'

'You can't leave us all destitute,' the mayor's lady protested. 'What can these poor people do?'

'Mebbe you can take 'em all back to Red Rock and raise a contribution for 'em? '

The train was chuntering along through the hill country, the sky darkening, the engineer and fireman unaware of what was happening behind them. Howling Wolf signalled to Pete and went ahead to climb over the tender of logs, hold his gun on them. Gradually they heard the locomotive screeching and hissing to a slow halt.

'OK, folks,' Pete yelled. 'I wanna thank you fer your contributions.'

'You good-for-nothing. ...' he heard Miss Baxter say, and, out of his eye corner, saw her draw a tiny derringer from her bag, fire spitting out, sharp pain catching him in the thigh.

He smacked her across the jaw with the back of his gloved hand and the derringer clattered down.

'Right,' he shouted, an anger of pain surging through

him. 'You're coming with us. Nobody try nuthin', I'm warning you. Or she gits it.'

He tumbled her out of her seat, pushed her out of the door, thrust his knee behind her to almost kick her onto the track. She stumbled, looking up at him, blood trickling from her nose. 'Move!' he shouted.

Howling was padding back alongside the track. Startled faces were looking out of the windows.

'What are you doing with that damn woman? We don't want her,' the Indian said. 'Baxter will pay to get her back. She's asked for it. Nearly blew my balls off.'

He looked with alarm at the blood wadding clammily through his britches. 'Get the hosses out.' He waved his six-gun up at the locomotive's passengers.

'Tell Baxter we want the heads of the men who killed thet Injin squaw. Otherwise he'll be gittin' a female head back in a box, his daughter's.'

'What are you, an Injin lover?' someone called. 'Thet ain't fair tradin'.'

'It's fair enough,' he growled. 'I wan' 'em thrown from the window of the train at this very spot. By these twin peaks. Two days from now. Or else. Otherwise send 'em alive and I'll do it myself.'

He jabbed his revolver at the girl. 'Move it, lady. You can ride the grey.'

THREE

'I musta bin crazy to bring this wildcat along.' Pete lay
with his pants down beneath a rock and watched
Howling Wolf tenderly apply a poultice of leaves and
herbs and plant juices to the raw bullet wound on his
inner thigh. 'She's only goin' to give us big trouble.'

'There,' Howling said, binding the mixture tight with
a piece of rag. 'I ain't sure this is going to work. My
grandmother showed me when I was a kid, but that sure
was a long time ago. White folk tried to knock all this
medicine outa me.'

'As long as it stops the bleeding,' Pete pulled his torn
and faded whipcords up. 'Guess it's goin' to be painful
ridin'. OK, miss, you can turn your head now. You ain't
missed much.'

She was lying down, her hands tied loosely to a tree
that hung over the rock by which they had made their
camp – in case she tried doing a vanishing trick in the
night. If she stole the horses with a little luck she might
make Connor's Crossing.

She snorted, contemptuously, as she watched him
buckle his leather belt, and poke at the small fire on top
of which a coffee pot was bubbling. This lean
long-legged Texan who had dared to strike her. A man
had never struck her before. And that applied to her

fiancé, John. He was the perfect gentleman. As to these scoundrels she doubted if they would have any qualms about what they did to her. She was going to have to try to prevent them attacking her, play one off against the other. Otherwise, she was ruined, socially. At that moment she was not even sure they might not kill her.

'You didn't have to kill that feller,' Pete said, handing Howling a tin cup of black coffee. 'He hadn't even got his gun outa the holster.'

'I wanted to,' the Wichita replied. 'I feel good about it. I wish I'd taken his scalp.'

'Look here, Henry, if you're goin' to hang around in my company it's no good talking like that. They didn't have nuthin' on you afore, apart from a little robbery, a few years in the pen. Now they gonna hang you.'

'They gotta catch me first. And how about you – kidnappin's a hanging matter.'

'They bin tryin' to hang me fer a long time. Once they damn near succeeded.' He jerked his neckerchief up and showed him the vivid rope burn on his throat. 'I bin expectin' it. Anyway, I'm gittin' along in years. What is it, thirty-five now. Say, that's old! Never fails to amaze me how I'm still alive. But, you're jest a boy. You got your life in front of you.'

He untied the young woman's hands and handed her hot coffee. 'Hyar! If ya ain't got no objections to usin' my mug. Guess it ain't like what your ladyship's used to.'

'Thank you,' she said, shaking some life into her fingers. 'You're not going to get away with this, you know. My father will raise the biggest posse south of the Arkansas River.'

'I don't think he'd better jest yet because we've got the ace – you.'

'You fools. If you had any sense you would see me safe to Connor's Crossing and disappear out of this territory.'

'They know my terms. I want the men who murdered Henry's sister. This is the only way of gittin' 'em as far as I can see. Prairie oysters to your taste?'

'What are they?' she asked, as he fished one out of the ashes and handed it to her, burnt and unappetizingly soft and wobbly in her palm.'

'Try it,' Pete said, giving a wink to Howling Wolf.

'Mmm!' she couldn't but help exclaim, biting into the flesh. 'Tasty.'

As they had ridden away from the railroad they had come across a bunch of young longhorns in a box canyon. They reckoned they would be doing whoever owned them a favour by gelding these youngsters, and they soon had them lassoed and thrown, and bellering plaintively, looking for their departed parts. It was a cowhand's favourite repast.

'Tell me,' Howling Wolf said, 'did you have this plan to avenge my sister before we got on the train?'

'No, it jest occurred to me after *she* tried to geld *me*.'

'You do not have to fight my battles for me. You can go. I will wait for the men to come.'

'You're my pal, aincha, Henry? Reckon you can do with a little support. Never know how many of them there's goin' to be.'

'There will be too many for both of you', Katherine said. 'You can't win.'

'It's a matter of honour. Guess you didn't think a thief and a redskin would know the meaning of that word?'

'You're a fool,' she said.

'Have another.' Pete offered another burnt testicle. 'Nice, ain't they?'

'Yes,' she agreed, daintily biting into it. 'What did you say it was?'

'Balls,' he said, and guffawed.

'Eugh!' She took a deep gulp, looked at the object in

her hand, tossed it back in the fire. 'I suppose that's your idea of a joke?'

'Sweetbreads you would know 'em as. You genteel folk have fabricated all kinds of words to disguise thungs from what they really are.'

'I'd like to go into the bushes, if I may?'

'Go. You ain't hobbled too tight. Don't worry, we won't peek.'

As they heard her rustling about Pete muttered, 'How the hell she's gonna sleep with thet arse cooler on God only knows.'

Howling Wolf's teeth flashed in the firelight, and, after a while, he said, 'Maybe it would be a suitable vengeance if I raped her and killed her? Then it would be over.'

Katherine stopped in her tracks, as, returning to the fire, she heard the Indian's words.

Pete turned to watch her. His thick hair was toned blue-black in the flames, and his eyes shone like dark gems. 'Thet ain't such a bad idea. She sure is a sassy little bitch. Shall we play a hand to see who does it? I ain't had a virgin for many a year.'

'You wouldn't dare. If you're trying to frighten me. ...'

Pete laughed, tipped his hat over his eyes, and produced a pack of cards. 'Tell me, were you aimin' for my manhood, or are you jest a lousy shot?'

'You crude, contemptible ... I thought the wonderful Confederates prided themselves on their chivalry.'

'Not toward Yankees we don't.'

'Have you not heard of the spoils of war?' Howling Wolf asked. 'This is one hand I intend to win.'

'You might as well make yourself comfortable, Katherine,' Pete drawled. 'Loosen your stays, if you like.'

She was going to reply to his effrontery, but her mouth had gone very dry, and she was not sure, for once in her life, what to say. Not sure whether they were teasing her, or serious. She did not want to make them mad and find out.

'After all,' Pete said. 'People are going to assume thet's what we're gittin' up to out here. So we might as well git on with it.'

Katherine looked anxiously around at the dark canyon walls. There was no hope of escape. Was this, she wondered, gong to be the sudden end of her life?

FOUR

'I don't know no law 'ginst shootin' an Indian,' the editor of the Red Rock *Reveille* said. 'Down south where our boys are fightin' the Apache they git paid bounty on every scalp they bring in. Why this feller's gotten so hellfire hot under the collar about some durn squaw fer's beyond me. And I'm goin' to say so in my editorial.'

'You ain't goin' to say no such thing.' Luther Baxter watched the bald-headed bigot in his green eye-shield and inky apron setting up a column, picking letters out from cases of lead type. 'You are going to say that the people of Red Rock try to live at peace with the Indians but a drunken frolic got outa hand ending with the squaw's unfortunate demise. The culprits were about to be dealt with by due process of law – ain't that right, Sheriff?'

'Uh?' The guardian of law and order, sprawled in a chair, jerked his big jaw off his ham fist, and came alive. 'Sure. You were goin' to fine 'em a week's wages weren'tcha, Mr Baxter?'

'Ignore that last remark, Mr Editor. The culprits have volunteered to go after the train robbers and bring them in.'

'They have?' The sheriff looked surprised. 'If that feller's the man I think he is he's mighty fast with a gun.

27

Them six boys of yourn ain't so hot, suh, no way.'

'So, who do you think he is?'

'This one.' The sheriff shuffled through a pack of 'wanted' notices. 'Wanted for bank robbery and homicide. Uses the crosshand draw. First thing I noticed, them two big .44's, the butts hung forward.'

'Black Pete Bowen.' Baxter studied the poster handed to him. 'Sure does fit the description. Fast is he? So, what? All he wants is the men who mussed-up the squaw. Seems a small price to pay for the life of Katherine.'

'It's slaughter,' the editor protested. 'Luther, this ain't the way to reward your employees. You should send for army assistance, have these miscreants rounded up. Kidnapping's a federal offence.'

'That's just what I don't want, some durn army commission poking its nose into our affairs. We've been allowed to get away with moving onto Indian land, elbowing 'em out, and me, you, we've all benefited. We've made our money buying cheap, selling dear to the railroad company. We don't need to advertise our methods or somebody in Washington might just start asking questions.'

'Well, no, Luther,' the editor said, hammering at a case of lead with a mallet. 'You've got a point there.'

'If you ask me it was that damn fool remark of yours in the editorial – "havin' fun with a squaw" – that well might have got this, this Bowen feller riled up. These kinda incidents happen, we all know, but they're best left unmentioned.'

'Waal,' the sheriff said, 'I got your boys rounded up and in the hoosegow like you said. Shall I march 'em over?'

'Do that, Sheriff. And remember, it's the life of my daughter that's at stake here. If one hair of her head is harmed by your inept bungling I pity you. Remember, Sheriff, it was you allowed those desperadoes to ride on that train with her.'

'Jeez, Mr Baxter,' the big, clumsy lawman stumbled to his feet, 'I never thought.'

'No, that's your trouble. That's the trouble with both of you.'

As he watched the sheriff hurry across the wide dusty main street to the gaolhouse Baxter tried to compose himself, control his seething anger and fear that anything might already have happened to Katherine. He took his pearl-grey, low-crowned Stetson off, and wiped back his wavy hair. He nervously touched the loose tie at the throat of his soft linen shirt and flicked dust from the silver facings of his grey frock coat. He was of German stock, with strong straight features. He had come out to these parts to farm, but had found it more profitable to dabble in real estate. He did not consider he had done anything particularly villainous. He was simply more astute than his fellow men. He had given people mortgages, and when the crop failed, it was unfortunate, he had had no option but to claim their land. Sometimes, naturally, they became obstreperous. That was why he was forced to employ a half-dozen beerhall yahoos and bully boys on his farm. Sometimes pressure had to be put on the more recalcitrant nesters to vacate their lands, to move along. Sure, there had been a little bloodshed, a little violence. No more than was necessary. It was the nesters' faults for resisting. He had not wanted his only daughter, Katherine, to think of him as a hard man.

Baxter had prospered in Red Rock. He owned large tracts of land, many properties. He had brought Katherine up in a fine mansion, with every solicitude, educated her as a lady. Since that day his Irish wife had run away he had devoted his life to his daughter. She was his pride and his joy. And now he was devastated – that anybody should dare do this to them.

The glass door of the newspaper office rattled open and six unshaven, surly men, their legs in irons, were prodded in by the sheriff and his rifle. They were lined up, their chains clattering, and stood, some defiantly, some guiltily, in front of Baxter.

'Well, boys, I hope you're proud of yourselves,' he said. 'I've been a good employer to you and this is how you repay me. The sheriff here has had orders to hang you all for the murder of that Indian gal,' – there were howls of protest – 'yes, murderers, that's what you are, and cowards. I don't care what race she was, she didn't deserve that.'

The boys looked at each other as if they were not hearing right. 'She was a damn squaw!' one said.

'OK, you were just having your fun and things went too far. I'm going to give you the chance to put things right. Those two desperadoes have got my daughter. They have said they are willing to fight it out with you. So, tomorrow you go out on the cars and you take them. Savvy?'

One of the men pouted his lips, querulously. 'Who is this feller? Some professional gunman? We ain't up to outshooting the likes of him. You know that.'

'Sure you are. The odds are in your favour. Six to two. And one of 'em's an Injun. The sheriff's been making enquiries. There's nothing on this Pete fellow. He's an amateur. Robbing a train for a few dollars. Anyhow, we'll be backing you.'

Others of the men grunted and snarled, but one said, 'Why can't you go after these two with a regular posse? Why us?'

'Because this is the way they want it. They're loco.

Some crazy idea, I can only assume, of avenging the Indian's sister. Remember, my daughter's life is at stake. So, you have no option. It's either this, or the rope. C'mon, you can kill 'em, boys.'

The men mumbled their protest, and the youngest of them threw himself at Baxter's feet. 'It wasn't me, Mr Baxter. I had no part of it.'

'You were there, weren't you?'

'I didn't do nuthin'. I only watched. It was them. They were all mad drunk.'

Baxter stepped forward and smacked him viciously across the face. 'You filthy crawling snake!' he screamed. 'Get on your feet. What are you? Do you call yourself a man?'

He dragged the youth to his feet, hurled him away, turned on his heel, and walked out of the office. 'Tomorrow!' he shouted, in parting.

They left the horses and mule in a makeshift corral of cottonwood poles in a hidden gulch with a stream running through for them to water, and climbed on foot back up to the railroad track and on up to the twin peaks hanging over them. The terrain was harsh coarse rock which cut into Katherine's thin-soled lady's button-sided boots and snagged her dress and stockings.

In the night she had discreetly dispensed with her bustle, and loosened her stays, as Pete suggested, to give her body more room to breathe. She perspired freely as she struggled up after the men, a noose loosely around her neck which the Indian gave a jerk to if she were laggardly. The sun rose higher in the sky and beat down upon them and she wished that she had had a more wide-brimmed bonnet than the silly pill box cap and veil perched on her red hair. At one point she slipped and screamed as a rock ripped her green silk dress, gashing it from the thigh. As she put a hand out to save herself the sharp stone cut her finger and blood flowed. 'What shall I do?' she cried.

'Suck it,' Pete growled. 'C'mon.' And he led them on up until they reached a dusty ledge where there was a small cave. 'This'll do,' he said. 'Makes a good lookout. Never know if they might send a posse out.'

'My father wouldn't risk my life. He will do as you tell him to do.'

'Yeah? For your sake let's hope so.'

He half-smiled as he looked the young woman over. She was hot, flushed, but still haughty. The gal wasn't a quitter. She'd got some gizzard. He'd gotta give her that. The dress and her white underthings had been ripped apart to reveal the top of her silk stocking and a sizeable piece of her pale plangent thigh. Her hair arrangement had collapsed onto one shoulder. She looked a mess, but kinda appetizing, too.

'You sure ain't dressed for this picnic.'

She noticed Pete's dark eyes flickering over her, scowled, and tried to patch her dress together. 'I hadn't planned on climbing mountains.'

'Siddown.'

They rested their backs in the shade of the overhang and Pete handed her his canteen. 'Don't go wasting none. That's all we got 'til tomorrow.'

His eyes raked along the railway line below and across the blue ridges of rock, hazy in the harsh sunlight. He wanted to get the lay of the land, avoid any surprise attack, plan an escape route.

'Henry's gone huntin'. Ain't much game up here. Don't reckon he'll have much luck.'

It was true. 'Guess I'm outta practice,' Howling Wolf said. 'This was all I could catch. ' He flung a rattlesnake down. 'Caught him coming out of his hole.'

'Eugh!' Katherine cried, once more, with a shudder. 'You're not going to eat that?'

'Sure thing,' Howling said, chopping off its head with his knife, starting to prise its coat off its still-wriggling body. 'Ain't you hungry?'

Katherine wet her lace handkerchief and wiped her face. 'Do I have to have this rope around my throat? I feel like an animal.'

The Indian's eyes dulled with desire and he grinned at her. 'That's the way I like a woman to feel, 'specially a white lady.'

Katherine edged away from him, uneasily. Pete glanced over at her. 'Sure, take it off fer now. It gotta go on again at night. Can't risk you running off on us. Or maybe trying to shoot us with our own weapons.' He looked at the sore wound on his thigh. 'Durn hellcat.'

'Indian nations over there,' Howling said, pointing vaguely towards the south-west. 'Maybe I go look for my people.'

'It's gunfightin' country, sure 'nough,' Pete muttered, and tipped out the haul from the train, counting the cash, dividing the watches and jewellery. 'Not a bad little haul. That's 30 dollars, five cents each. Gonna have to owe you five cents, Henry. All we need now's a pawnbroker's store.'

'I'm not selling this,' the Indian said, hanging Mr Mirick's gold watch and chain around his neck. He peered at the inscription. *For 30 years faithful service.*

Pete chawed on a plug of baccy and spat wryly. 'They find that on you they goin' to hang you.'

'Better than wear a damn reservation number. I wear what I feel like wearin'.'

And he clipped Katherine's amethyst drops to his ear lobes.

'You gotta point,' Pete said, and began building a

small fire from a bundle of dead wood he had carried
up from the creek. He put his can on to boil up tea, and
hung the snake and bacon over it to roast. 'Better keep
the fire low. No point in advertisin' ourselves.'

'Sometimes I think you got more Injun savvy than
me.'

'Should have. I known enough of you damn skunks.'

Howling Wolf stared venomously at him and wiped
his long-bladed knife on his palm. Pete wondered if he
took his jokes in good part. Since being together they
had developed a kind of mocking camaraderie, white
man against red, but since moseying into Red Rock and
finding his sister killed Henry Littlejohn had gone kinda
morose. He was becoming more like Howling Wolf. Pete
had fought against plenty of Comanche in his time, and
also alongside Cherokee and Kiowa, but he guessed he
would never understand the aborigine. Their moods
were subject to sudden change. You couldn't really
blame 'em, the way they had been treated. The Civil
War had given freedom to black slaves, but the red man
remained in servitude, abused and stolen from. Even
the civilized tribes of the nations had no rights to vote,
and never would have. They were kept apart.

'Huccome we finish that lil game of poker we were
havin'?' he said.

Howling Wolf had turned to the girl and was teasing
out her long strands of sun-glittering hair.

Katherine pulled away from him. 'Tell him to leave
me alone.'

'Sure.' Pete laconically dealt out the cards onto the
dust between them. 'You behave yourself, Henry. You
ain't been eddycated at that school out east to suddenly
turn native.'

'Is that so?' Howling said. 'Mebbe. I just tasted my first
white man's blood. Mebbe I taste my first white lady?'

'Mebbe.'

Pete hadn't been playing too well. He wasn't that great a poker man. And Henry sure was a crafty bucker. A man had to concentrate to master him. He had already won the matching amethyst ring, all the dollars and the bits and bobs and timepieces picked off the train passengers. Now there was only Katherine left to play for.

'Oh, my God!' she suddenly screamed. 'I wish you would get on with it. Anything would be better than this suspense.'

The two men durn near choked themselves laughing. 'You know,' Howling Wolf said. 'I reckon she really wants me.'

'Don't flatter yourself. Or you,' she darted a look at Pete, regretting her outburst. 'I'm just tired of your foolishness.'

'Waal,' Pete grinned. 'It's gittin' too damned dark to play any more. We better leave it 'til tomorrow.'

Pete stirred the embers of the fire and boiled up more tea, tossing a bit of charcoal in to settle the black mixture. 'How much sugar?' he asked Katherine. 'Sorry we ain't got no milk. Didn't pass no dairy.'

'You ain't goin' soft on her, are you?' Howling asked.

'Course I ain't,' Pete growled. 'She's only a woman.'

'We got a battle to come.'

'Iffen they come.'

'I go see if I can get the power. I don't wanna hang around with white folks.' Howling Wolf leapt away and in the clear starlit night went running and climbing up to the highest of the twin peaks, and, for hours on into the dawn, they could hear him whooping and howling and dancing, calling out to the heavens, to the spirits he had forsaken – the rhythmic and monotonous poetry of the red man.

FIVE

It was the waiting that got to him. The tension. The not knowing. The thinking they would come and they didn't come. The sun rising high, beating down on them as they hid in the bushes below the track, a trickle of sweat running down Pete's temple, down along his neck. It was high noon. If the locomotive had left Red Rock first thing in the morning it should be arriving soon. Or maybe they were coming by horseback? Maybe they had telegraphed for reinforcements from Connor's Crossing?

'C'mon,' he said, getting to his feet and dragging the girl with him across an open space of land towards a lone lightning-shattered tree 200 yards away from the track. He waved his rifle to Henry Littlejohn crouched in the rocks above the railroad, exactly beneath the twin peaks. And he tied Katherine to the tree with his lariat. Her seagreen eyes met his, something in them he did not understand: exhaustion, collusion, pity, he did not know. He did not tie her too tight. 'You gonna have to wait here.'

He clambered up to the track, and put his ear to the iron rail. He seemed to hear a faint singing sound. 'Hear that train a'comin',' he shouted. 'Comin' up the track. Comin' up from Red Rock. ...'

One thing was for sure, they would never take him back. Back to prison. Or to hang. He had determined long ago to go down fighting. One hanging had been enough. He slid through the scree back down the slope, ambled past Katherine, pale, in her torn dress, her back against the tree – hardly gave her a glance and took up his position. Yes, he could hear the sound of the engine getting closer now.

And there it was, the billows of smoke coming from the stack, coming round a bend and gradually huffing to a wheezing, wheel-locking halt beneath the twin peaks to stand strangely quiet. Now only a hiss and a growl from the 'Katie' engine was to be heard, the fireman hanging out, the clank of its bell. Its two carriages appeared to be deserted. And, more suspiciously, there were two enclosed goods vans. Pete didn't like the look of it.

After a while there was movement. A man, and another and, slowly, six in all, jumped down onto the track, one or two kneeling and looking warily around. They pulled six-shooters from their holsters and began to climb down towards Katherine. As they neared her Pete charged from the bushes on his grey mare, his reins gripped in his teeth, his rifle at his shoulder, firing rapidly, riding down upon them. And they panicked as Howling Wolf's rifle shots from the hillside caught two of them in their backs, spinning them into the dust. They were shouting and blazing away as Pete's slugs bowled over another two as he galloped through.

Howling Wolf bounded down the rocks and landed on the roof of the train. He leaned over and looked inside and saw a row of armed men crouched down in hiding, waiting for the signal to attack. He fired wildly at them, stood up and shouted at Pete, 'It's a trap! There's twenty of 'em inside.'

A bullet winged past Pete's cheekbone, burning it, another tore his shirt as, disconcerted, he wheeled his horse and faced the last two of the men who had raped the Indian girl. He spurred his horse and charged, and one of the men fired in his final frantic moments as Pete carefully aimed his Winchester and lodged lead in his guts, sending him sprawling with agonized cries.

At the same time, realizing they were discovered, some of the men in the train were blamming away through the train roof at where they believed the Indian to be. Others revealed themselves and took aim at Pete, their gunpowder crashing, bullets whining and ricocheting.

'This ain't friendly,' Pete muttered, through gritted teeth. He would have been willing to give the girl back. But this wasn't playing fair.

'Don't shoot,' Baxter screamed. 'I told you not to shoot. That's my daughter down there.'

But, when they saw the Indian leap from the train roof and hare towards Pete, they started blasting their carbines again.

Pete realized it had been Baxter's plan to wait until his daughter was safe before setting the men after them. He sent his horse chasing after the last of the rapists, a mere youth, who had run out of bullets and thrown his gun away. He lassoed him and dragged him behind the horse. He reached the girl, his frightened mare whinnying, her ears flattened, rearing in a cloud of dust, as he leaned over and slashd his knife across Katherine's bonds. And with one swing he hauled her up behind him to cover his back.

There was little the men could do but to hold their fire. And little the young woman could do but to hang on to the broad back of the outlaw to prevent herself from falling, as he hurtled away. With Howling Wolf hanging onto his stirrup they went flying down the slope to disappear into the shelter of the trees. The youth was dragged along behind.

'You fools,' Luther Baxter shouted, in chagrin. 'Get those horses unloaded. Get after them.'

SIX

They reached the corral where they had hidden the stallion, the Appaloosa, and the mule, and Pete told the kid to jump onto the stallion. He kept him tied to his saddle-horn and Katherine up back of him and they set off along a circular route he had espied from his eyrie on the Twin Peaks, only it wasn't as easy to follow from down here. They went pounding along the canyons, slowly descending towards the rushing creek the railroad from Red Rock crossed. Yes, his theory was correct, and, after an hour of hard riding, they saw the trestled bridgework rearing high above them. They hauled in their snorting and lathered animals on a stretch of sand and let them drink – but not too much.

'OK, you've had your vengeance,' Pete said. 'Are you satisfied? Or do you want *him*, too.'

The youth had slid from the black stallion and looked up with startled eyes. 'I didn't do nuthin' to her. I was jest there. I had to watch. It made me sick. I liked that squaw, that gal, I mean. She was pretty, but kept to herself. She worked late cleanin' folks' houses. That's when we caught her, they did, I mean. Please, you gotta believe me. Mr Baxter made me come.'

Henry shrugged, and Pete drawled, 'Sure, quit whining. You ain't no more to me than a gnat on a dog's dick. He won't scalp ya. It wouldn't be worth the bother. Anyways, I need ya. You gonna wait here for the posse. Or you can climb up there to the rail. Jest give Baxter a new message. His two-timin' sidewinder ways has gotten me mad. Now he's gonna have to pay if he wants his daughter back. Two thousand dollars in three days time. He's got plenty and it ain't honestly earned. And tell him next time, if he tries any funny tricks, she's gonna git a bullet in her head.'

Katherine flinched at this. She had been holding onto Pete's waist to steady herself, and she took her hands away like a scalded cat. She had lost her little cap, her red hair had streamed out in a tangle over her shoulders, and, sitting a'straddle, her dress was rucked up, her bare thigh, and torn pantaloons revealed.

'How does he pay you?' the youth said.

'You bring it. Alone. High noon. Three days from now. You stop on the other side of this bridge. Savvy? What's your name?'

'Davey, suh. Davey McPherson.'

'Waal, Davey,' – Pete unhitched the lariat from him, recoiled it – 'think yourself lucky we lettin' you go. Don't go rapin' no squaws no more.'

'No, suh. I certainly won't. Three days. I'll be here.'

'Let's git,' Pete yelled. 'Hee-yaugh!'

And he jerked the mare forward with such violence Katherine all but tumbled off. She had to hang onto his waist again as they followed the stream up into the mountains.

Davey was sitting on a rock by the creek beneath the towering wooden bridge when the posse rode up. Mr Baxter at their head.

'Which way have they gone?' he shouted.

'Up there.'

'It's all a maze of mountainous chasms up there,' the sheriff said. 'They might be headin' on into Indian Territory. Might take a week to track 'em down.'

Davey, not without some sense of importance, delivered Black Pete's message.

'Two thousand dollars!' Baxter exploded. 'The blackguard's crazy.'

'He said you shouldn' have two-timed him. You got him mad now,' Davey said. 'I think he'll kill her if he has to. He's a mean-lookin' hombre. The Injun's out for blood.'

'What did she look like – Katherine?' – Baxter's voice faltered – 'Was she bearing up?'

'Sure, she looked fine, only kinda wild. Her dress is all torn, showin' her legs. Not the lady she usually is. I wouldn' like to venture a guess what they bin doin' to her.'

'Shut your mouth, you whelp,' Baxter shouted, slashing his quirt across the youth's face. 'You repeat any talk like that you'll know my wrath.'

'We better git on after 'em,' the sheriff said, climbing back on his horse. 'They cain't go so fast with thet mule along.'

'No. It's too risky. I will pay them. When my daughter's safe I will hire some real gunmen to track these villains down. Not inept fools like you.'

The winter snows on the high Ozark Mountains had melted and the water came tumbling and crashing past them as they climbed higher up the ravine. By mid-afternoon they had reached a wide pool fed by a waterfall, and Pete said they would rest and cook up a meal. He set to building a fire and mixing some sourdough and sent Henry out to hunt.

'I must bathe,' Katherine said. 'I feel so filthy. Would

you be a gentleman and let me be by myself for a while?'

'Sure,' Pete glanced at her: she looked torn and windswept that was for sure. 'I got needle and cotton in my pack. You can stitch your dress.'

It was with a sense of relief Katherine went behind some big boulders, pulled off what remained of her dress, and, with a gasp, eased herself into the freezing water, kicking and splashing, and, hurriedly dragging herself out to dry in the hot sun on a flat rock. She looked around. They were not, apparently, going to bother her. So she pulled off her lace-fringed bodice and squeezed it out. She laid it with the dress to dry.

Pete did not believe they were being followed, but you never knew what those dang fools would do. Try to catch them by surprise, maybe. So when the fire had caught nicely and the billy had begun to bubble, he climbed up onto a rock to look back down the valley. There was no sign of movement.

He glanced down on the other side of the rock and saw Katherine sat there, head thrown back, eyes closed, as if worshipping the sun, her thrusting orbs of breasts exposed, pale moons, their pouting red nipples, her body the blue-veined white of the true redhead, her torn damp pantaloons clinging to her long legs.

'Hmph.' He cleared his throat, uneasily. Something strong in him prompted him to scramble down to that gal, throw caution to the winds. But, he remembered saying something to her about 'honour', that she didn't believe such as he and the Indian could possess. Honour! It brought vague memories of long ago, other times when he had believed in such words.

'Down, boy,' he muttered to his *membre virilis* (to coin Doc Johnson's term). He climbed down to his fire and the making of tea.

If he gave in to his animal instincts he would be no

better than the men all this fuss was about. Killing them had given him no satisfaction. It had left a bitter taste in his mouth. The sooner they got the ransom paid and handed her back 'intact' the better it would be. She was a damn good looker, none-the-less.

Howling Wolf, who was crouched down in the rocks on the other side of the pool, gave a low whistle as his eyes lingered lustfully on the half-naked Katherine. Who would have thought he could have a proud rich white woman like her. He didn't care about the ransom. He just wanted her.

He heard Pete rattle on the billy for tea. Saw him climb a rock and toss a blanket down to Katherine. Saw her look up, startled, and wrap it around herself. Saw her smile, mysteriously, to herself, pick up her garments and clamber back to the fire.

Henry hadn't had much luck, once more, with his hunting. He had been watching other game. But the chuckawallah lizard he had managed to catch, although not going down too well with the young woman, made a change to the usual cowboy fare of bacon and beans. They roasted it on a stick over the fire. Katherine sat there barefoot, her hair glistening wet and clinging to her forehead. She looked refreshed and relaxed.

The rushing of the water and the rustle of the wind at this height seemed to be as a dreamlike babble of voices, like the whisper of gods or ghosts in the boulders, but what language they were speaking she did not know. In spite of her predicament she was, at that moment, feeling good; the exercise, the mountain air, the excitement, even the shooting and violence had made her feel that she was really alive. And there was something about these two desperadoes, deplorable as they were, that was different to anybody she had met in Red Rock.

Black Pete was leaned back against his saddle by the waterside, rolling himself a cigarette as if he hadn't got a care in the world. And the Indian had pulled out a worn leatherbound book entitled *Plato's Death of Socrates*, which he was quietly studying as he puffed at a long carved stone pipe. She had not realized that an Indian could be interested in anything apart from hunting, whiskey and superstition.

'Henry was educated at college,' Pete said, as he saw her watching him. 'He came back in search of his roots. What he found was not very pleasant. His family dead, his tribe dispersed.'

'I'm sorry,' she said, 'about his sister.'

'You needn't talk about me in the third person,' Henry said, looking up. 'Didn't you know? It's not polite.'

'Is the book interesting?'

'Yes. I'm reading the Greeks. Those Hellenic times, they strike a chord in me. They have an affinity with the life of my people before the whites came. The tribal wars, the gods and goddesses, the restless searching for truth, when bravery and beauty and balance were held above all. The Greeks wrote it down. My people left no written history. We have only legends told by the shamans.'

'Yes,' – she was eager to agree – 'I see what you mean.'

'I don't see how you can. You white people only understand greed and money and destroying and grabbing land and killing; killing people, killing animals, the beaver, the wolf, the buffalo, destroying the bowtaut harmony of the natural world.'

And Henry Littlejohn's face hardened, his eyes like obsidian, his lips a razor-like gash, the face of Howling Wolf. 'I'll take first watch,' he said, picking up his rifle. 'I'll wake you when the moon begins its fall.' And he stalked off into the dusk.

'I think you've upset him.'

'Why?'

'I dunno,' Pete said. 'Before the whites pushed into Red Rock, before the war, Henry's family had a thriving tobacco farm there, their own black slaves, their own log buildings, shipping their produce by steamboat down the Arkansas. That was stripped from them. That red rock was sacred to them. I guess he's got a right to be mixed up and bitter.'

Katherine nodded. She had never thought of them as humans. Only savages. 'I guess so,' she said.

As night fell Pete pulled his greatcoat from the mule pack – the faded Confederate grey and threw his soogan to her. 'You can have my blanket. Make yourself a bed up in the rocks. I'll stay here by the fire.'

She noticed that he was not roping her any more. It was as if he trusted her not to run. She was grateful for that.

'Goodnight,' she called.

But, it wasn't a good night, for in the middle of it Pete heard a muffled scream, and woke to see two shadowy figures struggling up in the rocks. He got to his feet and grabbed his gun, and, approaching, saw that it was Howling Wolf on top of Katherine, bending low down over her head, doing something to her, and her coughing and choking and trying to push him off.

'You git offen that gal, you young skunk,' Pete shouted. 'You hear? Or you wanna hole put in your back?'

Howling Wolf stopped and turned, a knife in his hand, held by the blade. And he threw it at Pete's head.

Pete saw a flash of steel, and instinctively ducked. The knife clattered off a rock.

'I'm gonna forget you did that, Henry. Now git offen her, pronto.'

Henry did so, looking into the hole of Pete's .44 backing away, reaching for his rifle. 'It's only because she's a white woman. You don't want an Indian touching her. You're all the same.'

'Throw that over here. You can have it back in the morning when you've cooled down a bit.'

Henry reluctantly tossed the rifle to him. 'Yeah, I know what you're up to. You want her for yourself. I've seen you looking at her.'

'Sure I want her. Any red-blooded man would do. She's a fine looking squaw. But we can't jest take her. Don't you see, it would be the same thing as happened to your sister? We would be betraying *her*.'

'Look at my dress,' Katherine said, angrily, trying to cover her breasts. 'It's just a rag now.' And she started to cry, as if a dam had burst, the tears flowing from her.

'See what you done,' Pete said. 'I jest cain't abide a cryin' woman. Come on, Katherine. It's okay. He ain't gonna hurt ya. He's jest a mite frustrated. He's a growin' boy.'

'A mite?' the Indian said. 'I'm crazy for her.' And he turned and stalked away into the darkness, and pretty soon they could hear him up on the crags – howling to the moon.

SEVEN

They moved camp the next day, circling along the ledge of the mountain, Howling Wolf sullen and sulking, not speaking to them.

'There's a cave up there we could hide out in,' Pete said, towards midday. 'Give us some shade from the sun. You wanna go take a look, Henry?'

The Indian grunted and nudged his Appaloosa up a steep track through the rocks. They saw him jump down to enter the cave. There was a whinnying scream. The pony reared up, flailing its hooves. A large mountain lion was slashing her claws across Henry's chest. She whirled to attack the pony which stumbled back over a rock, pitched over, crashing down the mountain-side. Snarling and spitting the lion sank her fangs into the retreating Indian's leg.

Pete yanked out his Smith and Wesson, but did not dare fire too close for fear of hitting his friend. He loosed three shots over the struggling pair. The lion, alarmed, ceased her attack and slunk back into the cave.

Howling Wolf was groaning, his face a rictus of pain. Pete reached him and saw his velvet shirt was shredded. Cruel crimson claw marks lacerated his ribs. His knee was torn open and bleeding profusely.

Black Pete peered into the cave. He didn't fancy going

in there. She was obviously a female defending her young. And it was more important to get Henry away and attended to. 'Hang onto me. Try to hop on your other leg. We gotta get you down from here.'

Katherine was trying to soothe the Appaloosa pony, which was lying there, terror in its bulging eyes, making vain attempts to get to its feet.

'Looks like it's broke its back or somethun. There ain't nuthun' we can do for it. You better look the other way.'

Pete put his revolver to the animal's temple and fired. The bullet smashed through the creature's brain and it slumped dead. 'The lion can have you.'

They managed to get Howling Wolf to hang over the grey, and they moved him along the mountain for a mile or so until they found a small overhang that gave shade and from which water trickled. The Indian cried out with agony as they laid him down, beads of sweat pricking out on his brow.

Pete ripped up part of the Indian youth's torn shirt and tied it as a tourniquet to try to staunch the profusely trickling blood. Katherine made a pillow of a blanket for his head. Pete took his canteen and tried to wash the wound, cutting away the ripped clothing. The lion's teeth had gone clean through the loose flesh of the calf and had taken a mess of a piece out of the knee.

'Hot damn,' Pete whistled. 'You gonna have one hell of a stiff leg from now on.'

It occurred to him they might be needing a surgeon to amputate. 'First she tries to blow my balls off. Now this. Wish I'd never set eyes on Miss Katherine Baxter. Wish I'd never gotten us into this whole damn fool thung.'

'Wish I'd never left the east,' Howling Wolf said, and tried to grin. 'You can keep the damn west.'

'Only thing I got is some iodine. Used it in Colorado for the frostbite. It's gonna hurt like hell. Ain't as good as whiskey, but it should keep the maggots from gettin' at ya. You better git ready to bite on the bullet, Henry.'

Pete found the bottle in the pack. Howling Wolf braced himself and shuddered as the iodine scalded him. Pete shook his head, sadly, and dosed the wound once more. He cut up a blanket and tied the strips tightly around the wound. 'Guess that's about all I can do. You ain't goin' to be able to walk very well for some while. Maybe I can fashion you a crutch? If I can find a tree.'

They had climbed high and there was very little foliage around. From their eyrie they could look out from the mountain chain to a distant savannah of grass, forest and lake. Pete went in search of wood and managed to find a small copse in a gully.

'I got you a hickory crutch and some firewood. I'll bile up some tea.'

It occurred to him that in their absence Katherine could have got on the stallion and made her escape. Maybe that would have been the best end to this affair. Maybe he wanted her to. Maybe it hadn't occurred to her. She seemed to be as concerned about Henry as he was.

'Never thought I'd see a gal like you fussin' over an Injin.'

'I have feelings – the same as anyone.'

'An Injin who tried to rape you last night?'

'You stopped him.' Her green eyes interlocked with his. 'Didn't you? I think you have decent feelings, too.'

'Don't count on it.'

'Hey, I sometimes get the feeling you two like each other,' Howling Wolf said, grimacing as he pulled himself up against a boulder.

'Don't count on it,' Katherine said. 'I'm your prisoner, am I not?'

'You sure are,' Pete muttered. 'But I ain't sure what I'm going to do about you now. We're goin' to have to hang around for a coupla weeks 'til Henry's able to move.'

Howling Wolf had almost got over the shock, and, as he sipped the sugary black tea that Pete gave him, in spite of the throbbing in his knee, he was beginning to see things clearly.

'You ain't hanging around here. If this knee gets gangrene I'm just as likely to die, anyway. And if you don't turn up in the morning with her they are going to come looking for us. And it won't be long until they find us here.'

'So?'

'So, I'm ready to take my chances against the lions, or the posse, or whatever.'

The mule gave a loud agonized bray at this point, as mules are wont to do.

'They'll soon find us if he does that all the time,' Pete mused. 'Henry, have you any objections to us eating your Appaloosa?'

'His spirit has flown now. He is just dead meat.'

'So, why leave him to the lions and vultures? I'm goin' to go carve us a few pony steaks.'

An hour or two later, after he had roasted the steaks over their fire and they had all eaten their fill, Katherine went to do whatever she had to do behind some rocks, and Pete took the opportunity of her absence to say: 'I bin thinkin', what you said makes sense. I'm gonna leave some cold steaks. You got water here. You should be able to last a week or two, and maybe by then your leg will be on the mend. Jest lie low and there ain't no reason why they should find you. I'm gonna have to leave soon, get halfway down the mountain before nightfall, and go to meet young Davey in the morning.

Once I've made the transaction – if I'm still in one piece – I'll go on, try to draw anyone following away from you. I reckon they'll want to go after the man with the money. They ain't bothered about an Injin. And I got a tempting price on my head.'

'That's all very well,' Howling Wolf said. 'What about my share?'

'You've already got the jewellery and ready cash. Your safest bet would probably be to head on into Injin Territory, find your clan. But, if you're such a greedy son-of-a-gun, you can come looking for me.'

'Where you gonna be?'

'I'll follow the railway on to Connor's Crossing.'

'You'll wait for me there?'

'Yup. Unless there's trouble, some of 'em on my tail. If so, I'll try and head west.'

'You sure you'll wait?'

'I'll wait as long as I can, Henry. I'm goin' to leave you Jesus. He's a hundred-dollar stallion. You take care of him, you hear.'

Howling Wolf nodded, glumly. 'Well, at least I got some readin' material with me. I never did get to the end of that book. I'm gonna have plenty of time now.'

'You sho' are, Henry.'

'So, don't go spending my share. I ain't never had a thousand dollars in my hands. Nor a hundred-dollar horse under me.'

'We never did finish that game of cards, did we?' Pete smiled as he saw Katherine climbing back up to them. 'Here she comes.'

'You old bastard. I knew you were holding out on me.'

'Your day will come, Henry. There's a lot of good wimmin in this world.'

'Go, Black Pete. Go. Maybe we will meet in the happy hunting ground. You have been a good friend to me.

You have taught me to be a warrior.'

'Let's hope we meet before then, Henry.' Pete stuck out his gloved hand and gripped the youth's. 'You know, Henry, I don't reckon you're ever going to make a good Indian. You've got too much of the white man in you.'

Howling Wolf raised his palm and said, 'Be gone, Paleface,' and smiled, widely.

Pete looked at Katherine. 'C'mon, gal. Git on the mule. You an' I got an appointment to keep in the morning.'

EIGHT

'Once my daughter's safe you go after them. Is that understood? You get the 2,000 dollars back, you keep it. That's your payment. Fair enough? I just want them dead. Anyone who's done this to my daughter deserves to die. There's a 1,000-dollar reward on the white man outstanding in Texas. He walked into the Cattlemen's Club, murdered that cattle baron, Murchison, cool as a cucumber. There's a 500 reward on him in Kansas for bank robbery. The railway's put up 250 on each of 'em for this last train hold-up. So you stand to collect 5,000 dollars in all. How many men do you want in the posse?'

'I don't,' the man spat out the words. 'I work alone. And I need another 1,000 before I start. You think you can git outa payin' me?'

'But you'll get the 2,000 ransom.' Baxter was unnerved by the man's unflinching eyes boring into him out of a bearded weatherbeaten face. 'Surely that's enough?'

'No. What if he ain't got it by the time I catch up? That'll mean I get nothing outa you. You gotta pay for killin'.'

Baxter sniffed. The bounty hunter's ripe odour was worse than that of a buffalo hunter. He was a huge grizzly of a man wearing dead rats and bloody scalps, armed to the teeth with guns and bandoliers of bullets.

He made him feel uneasy, if not almost queasy. But he was supposed to be the best there was, the fastest bar none. He was a famed Indian fighter, with an intense hatred of all redskins since his family had been wiped out by them when he was a boy. He was known simply as The Indian Killer. He had arrived on the train into Red Rock in answer to Baxter's telegraph to Dodge City. He had been lucky to get him. This was a man who would track the worst desperado down to the end.

'What the hell you do with all the money?' Baxter grumbled, as he went to his safe.

'That ain't your problem. Your problem is to pay. That's my price. The price of doin' you squirmy coyotes' dirty work.'

He's got dead eyes, Baxter thought. He would just as soon shoot me down. He slapped the 1,000 dollars onto the desk top. The Killer picked it up and stamped his way out. The whole house seemed to shake.

NINE

The sun was falling, but it was still hot when they reached the cascading stream where they had camped the night before. They were dust-grimed and sweaty, and the sun had burned Katherine's nose, her pale skin and almost bare thighs. Pete dismounted to let the mule and the grey mare water. Katherine looked at the placid pool of water and, although she knew it was madness, she had to say it, 'Oh, I wish I could bathe again.'

Pete looked at her and smiled, 'Go ahead.'

Katherine felt quite dizzy at the thought of what might occur, alone there with this man. But he had not pestered her so far, the card game had only been a joke, surely? She could trust him. In the West the ordinary cowhand had a high regard for what few white ladies there were, a sense of propriety. And, as she went behind the rock and stripped off what remained of her dress, she felt somehow excited, breathless with the daring of what she was doing. What would folks say in Red Rock if they could see her? They were probably saying some pretty nasty things, anyhow.

The coldness of the clear water made her gasp, but she gritted her teeth, and swam around, and washed the dust from her hair. She was completely naked as she did not want to get what was left of her clothes wet, and the water tingling against her body was beautiful. Suddenly there was an ungainly splash as Pete, stark naked, too, jumped off the rock and landed in beside her. He sank to the bottom and came up under her as Katherine screamed and tried to swim to the shore. But he had her in his strong arms.

'Thought I'd jine you,' he grinned. He kissed her lips, savagely. Katherine tried to struggle, but something within her made her respond.

They kissed until they began to shiver, and they crawled, like two lizards, out onto the shelf of flat rock, and, without speaking, her eyes on his, Katherine lay down, and Pete climbed on top of her, his mouth slipping to her wet and shining white breasts, their pert aureolas. Soon they were naturally enjoined.

'Oh, my God, yes, yes, yes. ...' She heard herself saying. There was no way she could stop.

Afterwards they lay back and dozed and dried their bodies in the warm sun. Katherine reached her hand out and her fingers stroked his bullet-scarred skin, his lean ribs. 'It wasn't the first time for me,' she said. 'I did it in the barn when I was fourteen with one of the hands. He got fired. It's the first time since.'

As they sat beside the fire in the dusk Katherine snuggled into his greatcoat. 'I don't want to go back to Red Rock,' she whispered. 'I don't want to go to Connor's Crossing. Can't you take me with you?'

'You must be crazy, woman,' Pete laughed. 'They wouldn't let you do that. Anyway, I'm depending on that 2,000 dollar ransom.'

'You cold-hearted bastard,' she said and pulled herself away from him.

TEN

In the noonday heat Katherine sat on a rock by the iron railroad on the south side of the big trestle bridge that spanned the ravine. 'Chu-chu-cha … chu-chu-cha … chu-chu-cha!' They heard the 'Katie' engine approaching, louder and louder, its smoke stack belching black clouds. They saw the front of its boiler and its wide cow catcher appear from around a bend, the engineer in his goggles hanging from the cab. They heard a hiss as the steam brake clamped, the wheels squealed, and the locomotive slowly came to a halt at the far side.

'Right on schedule,' Pete growled, as they listened to it quietly spitting and susurrating, and saw the youth, Davey, jump down onto the track, a canvas bag in his hand. 'And it looks like he's delivering the goods.'

He cocked his six-gun and stood out in the middle of the track, taking her with him, his hand on her elbow. She stood there in her ragged dress, scratched, windswept, somehow defiant, and watched the youth approach over the bridge.

'Two thousand green backs in used notes, like you said.' Davey proffered the bag.

'Take it out and count it.' Pete squinted along at the ominously still train. 'How many men they got in there?'

'I come alone!' Davey did as he was bid and handed

the notes over. 'We goin' back to Red Rock. You okay, Miss Baxter?'

She ignored him and gave Pete a long cool regard as he grunted, 'Git goin'.' And she began to walk back across the bridge.

Davey hovered, nervously. 'There's a man in there. The Injun Killer they call him. He's vowed to git you.'

For moments a coldness seemed to paralyse Black Pete. The Indian Killer. He had heard of this man. His name reeked of blood. He wondered whether to face him out there and have it done with. But, he did not know how many more men might be on the train. 'Thanks,' he muttered, and Davey began to hurry back after Katherine.

Pete waited until they were nearly at the other side, then he knelt down and, with his cheroot, lit the fuse wire he had laid. He watched it fizzle across the bridge, saw Katherine reach the train. He stuffed the dollars into his shirt as a bulky, shadowy figure jumped down, a rifle in his hands. Pete jumped behind a rock as a bullet spanged past his head and ricocheted away.

'The bastard knows how to shoot,' he muttered.

The bridge erupted with the dynamite he had tied to its struts – timbers, rocks, iron rails, flying through the air, toppling into the chasm far below. Pete took advantage of the screen of billowing dust to hurry back along the track to where he had left the grey and the mule. He hauled himself into the saddle and with a last anxious look back went galloping away towards Connor's Crossing.

Katherine ran forward to look at the twisted tracks, the settling dust, at the menacing-looking gunman in his strange garb.

'The Indian's up there,' she said, pointing towards the hill.

The man turned his bloodshot eyes on her, a ferrety reek emanating from him.

'The Indian?'

'Yes, he's injured.'

'I'll get him first,' the man said, licking his cracked lips as if in expectation of a meal.

ELEVEN

Pete camped out overnight and sighted Connor's Crossing early the next morning. It was a collection of log cabins, shanties and tents on a bend of the muddy brown river which was in full flood. It was probable the news of the train robbery and kidnapping had reached here days ago and if he had any sense, he would give the place a wide berth and keep on running. But he had got tired of forever running, and he knew the Indian Killer wouldn't give up even if he had to follow him all the way to Arizona. And he knew the Indian Killer hunted his bounty alone, so it was doubtful there would be a posse. He had told Henry he would wait for him and he wasn't about to abandon his friend, and anyway he reckoned he could handle himself with any of the train construction gang. And, sooner or later, he would have to take a stand against his pursuer and this was as good a place as any. None-the-less, he naturally felt nervous as he watched the men teeming like ants completing the construction of the wooden bridge across the river, and pushing the rails on towards Texas.

In the years of being on the dodge, in his wanderings in Missouri and Kansas, trying to do honest work as a guide or cowpuncher before being forced to move on and take to dishonest occupations – like being a hired

gun or bank robber – Pete had become inured to the
idea of sudden and bloody death. Plenty of men, good
and bad, had tried but they hadn't succeeded. He wasn't
as young and as fast as he once was, and he knew the
odds were running out. One of these days a bullet was
going to get him. He was pretty certain of that. So he
hardened himself, and nudged the grey forward down
the slope razed of its lumber, towards the cabins, ready
to shoot and run again, if he had to.

He ambled his horse slowly through the tents and
shanties where ugly-looking women camp followers,
wives and doxies and their scruffy children, were
chattering, washing shirts, stirring at pots on smoul-
dering fires, or idly sat smoking their pipes. They eyed
him, curiously, the tall man in his tattered macinaw and
grey hat who rode through.

The largest of the log cabins had once been Connor's
store when only a creaking raft crossed the river, and his
customers were mainly trappers and Indians. Now it
had been turned into a bustling saloon where a
professional gambler and his whores plied their trade.
Nearby cabins housed stores, bank, railway office, forge,
boarding house, eatery and stage-coach agency. There
was a well-built hotel and other makeshift endeavours of
rough planks leaned one against the other, such as the
barber shop and bath house, pawnbroker's, gunshop,
and fancy clothing outfitter's.

Pete reined in outside the saloon. There were few
horses about because most of the gangers were Irish
townies, who had been brought in on the railroad
wagons. Just half a dozen horses were hitched to the rail,
standing looking pissed off in the noonday heat, flicking
their manes and tails at the flies. A couple of tame
Indians were sat on the boardwalk, huddled in their
blankets, going through a bottle of whiskey. They

looked like Pawnees. Pete loosely tied his grey mare and mule alongside, jerked his Winchester from the saddle boot, tucked it under his arm, and stepped up to the cabin door. Before entering he pulled his twin revolvers, one after the other, cocked them, squeezed the triggers, and moved each empty chamber around. A cowboy generally kept his guns like that if he was hard riding, in case of accidents. Now they were primed and ready to use. He spun them on his fingers, thrust them butts-forward back in his greased holsters, winked at the braves, and went inside.

In the gloom he could barely make out the faces and figures of some twenty or so men, most of them sat around a table beneath the familiar Bengal tiger sign where a game of faro was in progress. Others stood at the rough-sawn bar, getting stuck into the barrels of whiskey, rum and beer. The big-gutted mine host, known as Frenchie, was in mid-flow of animated banter with them when Pete entered. As he did so all conversation ceased and they turned to give him the look over. By their dusty clothes most seemed to be railgang boys, and only half a dozen were armed. There were a couple of trappers in coonskin caps and tattered buckskins, carrying old-fashioned muzzle-loaders and horns of powder. And four men with more modern weapons tucked into their belts. They were dressed in a citified way, their trousers tucked into muddy riding boots. Pete guessed they acted as heavy mob for the rail road company. Sprinkled among the men, sprawled lazily in eel-skin dresses, rouged and powdered, were several 'prairie nymphs'.

Pete scowled at the four company men. It was them he would have to keep in his sights.

'Howdy,' he muttered, and, spurs clinking, sauntered forward towards the bar, his hands ready, if necessary, to draw.

Frenchie, in checked shirt, woollen underwear, and fur cap, made no move to serve him, standing imperiously with his arms folded. 'Where you from, buddy?'

'Don't rightly see that's any business of yourn,' Pete said, pulling off his gloves. 'Gimme a drop of thet whiskey.'

'There been bad trouble up along the line,' Frenchie said. 'Shootin' and killin'. You come that way?'

'What line?'

'That line. The one that go to Red Rock.'

'Red Rock? Where's that?'

'Seventy miles away up the end of that line. Don't be funny with me.'

'Waal, excuse me, but I ain't never heard of it. Is that a crime? So happens, I've come along through the Nations from Fort Sill. Mighty pretty scenery. Damn Injins got themselves some mighty fine land.'

'Not for long they ain't.'

'How's that?'

'They ain't gonna be able to hang on to it for ever. Why 'ja think we putting this line through here?'

'Thought it had been given 'em in perpetuity. Now, am I gonna git thet whiskey or not?'

'What would be your business, stranger?' one of the railroad men asked.

'Don't recall that being any of your business, either. But, so happens my last job was guide to an English lord and his missus on a hunting party. Sure was toffee-nosed types.'

'Yeah?' another man growled. 'Smells kinda fishy to me.'

'You men think I had anything to do with that shootin' and killin' you're talking about, you had better think again. I ain't seen a soul for weeks. Last two fellers

I saw were a coupla government surveyors back in the mountains.'

'Yeah, we bumped into them, too,' one of the trappers chimed in.

'You did? What a coincidence!' And it *was*, because the two Pete had been thinking of he had met ten years before. 'So that proves it. Do I pass muster?'

'I reckern so,' Frenchie said, and reluctantly filled a glass from the barrel.

Pete studied it for seconds, then tossed it back. He winced and shook his head. 'Jesus! What you call this stuff?'

'Knock 'Em Dead,' one of the railmen laughed. 'Frenchie's home brew. He allus chucks a piece of rotten meat in the tub. Guaranteed to stop you in your tracks at fifty yards.'

'Gimme a bottle,' Pete said. 'I'll take my chance.'

Frencie filled him a bottle and passed it along. The men watched Pete saunter over to a seat by the small cobwebby window, and ease his bones, his rifle across his knees, the trigger guard close to hand. They didn't like the look of him, but none was particularly keen to argue about his story. They turned back to their chatting, drinking and gambling.

'C'mon, gents, place your lil bets,' the dealer called. And this they did as he flipped out the cards. He was obviously a professional by the cut of his frock coat, embroidered silk waistcoat, his cleanshaven cadaverous face and his dark hair slicked back. He too was pretty slick, but Pete couldn't see any sign of a crooked deck.

'Hi, handsome!' one of the girls called, giving a gap-toothed grin. Her hair was knotted and tousled, and she was wearing only a grimy chemise, and wrinkled black stockings held up by yellow ribbons. She was certainly not the most handsome of the bunch. She looked like she had just got out of the sack. She stood, unsteadily, and tottered on high heels over to him, to sit alongside. 'Gonna buy a girl a drink?'

'Nope,' he said, and refilled his own glass. 'I ain't in the mood right now.'

'C'mon, cowboy. How about I give you a nice bath, tickle your balls?'

'Look like you could do more with one yourself. Piss off, will you?'

'Arr, be like that, misery-guts. What are ya, one of them nancy boys?'

Pete gave a scoffing laugh. 'You could say that!'

He looked the other girls over. None of them was particularly toothsome. At least not to him right that minute. They were hook-nosed, or cross-eyed, tight-lipped, hard and shifty looking. They would skin you of your last ten cents, if they could. One fat old haybag looked eighty, if she were a day. She kept pacing back and forth, occasionally pausing to scratch tenderly at her meat, as if it were the only possession of value she had in the world. Perhaps it was.

Pete had nothing against prostitutes. He had known plenty of them in his time, especially since going on the lam. All shapes and sizes and colours and ages, and some of them were very pleasant and skilled at their job, some were pretty nasty characters and some really did have hearts of gold. But, for some reason, he always seemed to fall for high-class ladies, in the same way he preferred thoroughbreds to hacky old cow ponies. He took a sip of the whiskey and remembered Louisa, his lovely Spanish wife, who they had killed when they ran him off his land. He had not fallen for anyone for a long time after that, and had mostly kept company with loose women. Not until Lady Lucy, the English lord's wife came along, but she was more like a high-class nymphomaniac. He smiled to himself, wondering where she had gotten to and whose pants she would be getting into. Her butler's, probably. And, only this winter past he had bumped into that talkative little bluestocking, Isobel Sparrow, when he had gone on an assignment as hired killer to Silverillo in the Rockies. He had felt real affection for her, and would have been ready to marry her and settle down, but they came from different worlds. She had shamed him into fighting on the side of the men he had been hired to destroy, and they had crossed Bear Mountain together in winter, which no white man or woman had been known to have done before, chased out of Colorado by the vigilantes. It had, of course, been impossible. She had returned to Boston and her books and he had continued to wander. But she had changed him a lot. He was not so hard and cynical as he had been, and he had begun to enjoy life, Howling Wolf's amusing company and each day as it came. And now, this other haughty young woman, Katherine Baxter, had gotten under his skin. What if he had let her come along with him? Why couldn't he be content with one of these, with a Rat-faced Nellie?

'Waal,' he muttered, as the scrawny young hussy gave up on her salacious suggestions and wandered back to the card players, 'I gotta keep on my guard.' But a man couldn't be on guard all the time. Sometimes he just had to sleep and drink and get drunk and fornicate. Aw, hell, he mentally groaned. That ain't such a bad idea. And he poured himself another large glass of the Knock 'Em Dead. He knew that once he'd started on the bottle it was going to be a hard job stopping.

For the moment he was content to relax and watch the card players, trying to resist joining them. His faro was no better than his poker. He didn't want to lose all of his 2,000 dollars in one go. He listened to the clink of silver dollars, the men at the bar talking, the call of the dealer, and slipped easily into a semi-drunken reverie. All those girls, the places he had ridden through, the men he had killed, good men, bad men, he had lost count of the number. The men who had tried to kill him, the cattle baron's sons who had tried to hang him after they had killed his wife, his friend, burned his ranch house down, left him hanging on the end of a rope until his young son cut him down. He remembered his wife's unfaithfulness with his friend while he was away on a cattle drive, but he felt no bitterness towards her, only sorrow. He tried to imagine what his son would look like, seventeen now, wondered if he and his aunt had got the last (honest) money he had sent them. Did they ever think about him? He guessed you wouldn't exactly feel proud to have a no-good outlaw as your father. And suddenly, he tired of the melancholy drift of his thoughts, his lonesomeness, picked up the bottle and got to his feet, leaning his rifle against the wall. Maybe he would try the faro game, after all.

At that moment one of the men at the table, a shortish, grey and grizzled fellow with white stubble on his chin, gave a groan of despair, put his head on his hand and said, 'I'm done for boys. That's the farm gone. That's all I own.'

His body was stooped and his face tanned and lined by years of hard labour, but he seemed to visibly shrink even more. His whole personality, from being one of eager hope, seemed to totally collapse. He wore a dusty dark suit tucked into riding boots and a collarless shirt. He feverishly sought in his pockets, hoping he might have a dollar left, but it was no good.

The dandified dealer, his face unconcerned, scooped the silver coins in and crooned, 'Hurry it along, gents, place your lil bets. Don't hog that chair, suh, if you're through.'

Reluctantly the man eased himself from the chair, crammed his straw sombrero on his head and moved listlessly towards the door. He looked like he had been sitting there a long time. He had a bitter and forlorn look on his face as he took one glance back. He should have been a fine warning to anybody not to be lured into the game.

But Pete pulled a fistful of dollars out of his shirt, paid for the whiskey and said, 'I'll take that chair.' Although he preferred poker, blackjack or roulette, the main attraction of faro was that the player, or sucker, had virtually an even break. There was no thirty-six to one, with the added zero and double zero to buck as in roulette. Faro resolved itself to the simple matter of betting any card of the thirteen denominations from ace to king to win or lose. There were other ramifications but little scope for the dealer to cheat. This probably accounted for its popularity among the more ordinary folk in the West who had got kinda sick of being skinned by professional card sharps. They could satisfy their gambling fever and be in with a chance. But a man could still go down hard. In Colorado Pete had seen vast sums in silver ore, dust and nuggets being won and lost (won mainly by the house). He had heard tell of huge ranches being gambled away in one game. He had known a deputy who had pawned his revolvers to get back into one! And it was said the governor of New Mexico had gambled the state as his stake! Fortunately, he won. So the loss of a farm wasn't something you were expected to moan about.

'C'mon, gents, string along.' The dealer flipped the cards from the box and Pete and the others vied to place their bets. After a while he remembered the mare, and beckoned a small half-breed boy over. 'Is there anywhere I can stable a horse in this town, son? There's a grey and a mule outside. You reckon you can handle them? Here's a dollar. OK?'

'I can handle them better for two,' the boy grinned. 'Give them rub-down. There's no horse I can't handle.'

'Two it is. Proper lil businessman, aincha? You remind me of somebody I know.'

He poured them all a whiskey. 'Howzat, gents?'

Might be handy to make some friends. He made sure not to turn his back on the men with the guns.

TWELVE

Seven hours later Pete was five hundred dollars richer than he had been when he began. Lady Luck sure had been kind to him this day. It seemed like he couldn't lose. But, he was getting stiff and kinda hungry.

'I'm pulling out now gents,' he drawled, pushing back his chair. 'Anywhere I can get a bite in this place?'

'Sure, down the road.'

He stood groggily, knocked back the last drop in the bottle and hitched up his guns. The dealer, the trappers, and a couple of gamblers eyed him, the .44s, the long bowie knife of finest Solingen steel stuck in his belt, his long lean body. They eyed each other. Sometimes a man could be persuaded not to leave. None seemed to be in any mind to stop his departure. He looked a hard-bitten hombre, that was for sure.

His spurs clattered as he went to pick up his rifle, and made for the door. He was surprised to find it was already getting dusk. The construction men were coming in from the bridge work, wet and muddy and ruddy-faced. Those men really worked. He could smell food cooking at the camp fires. Most of them lived on credit until the job was done, and, after deductions of what they owed, had just about enough to go looking for another job. The first stars were sprinkling on. The men did not pay him much heed, but were hurrying to the saloon, or their tents, or to seek food.

The man who had lost was lying on his side on the wooden slatted sidewalk. He looked like he might be asleep but when Pete passed he saw that his eyes were open and staring into space. It looked as if he were frightened to go home, if any home he had. He looked like he had lost all hope.

'That's the way it goes,' Pete muttered to himself. 'There's him lost everything he had. And me, who's got plenty, increased my pile. A durn topsy-turvy world.'

But, what could you do? He relit his cheroot, pulled his hat down over his eyes, leaned his rifle carelessly on one shoulder, and went to take a look at the little town.

Along past the stores and big painted hotel the street trickled out in a mess of market stalls. At one, over a charcoal brazier, frijoles were being cooked, and the sharp scent, reminding him of southern Texas, attracted him across. He paid for a couple and chewed into them with gusto. They were damn hot, but certainly an improvement on Henry's cooking. Some Indian women, their faces creased like carved mahogany by the weather, were sat on their rush mats, one with a pathetic collection of limp fruit, berries and vegetables, others with lamp-holders and suchlike junk made from tin cans, and others purveying beadwork and blankets. They did not seem to be doing much business. There was a resigned air of patience about them. They would probably sit there all night. At the end of the row was a horse and wagon, and a pile of melons. A fair-haired girl of about seventeen was sat on the shafts of the wagon, an agitated look marring her sweet features. She was wondering what had happened to her father. She guessed he had started gambling again, but he had forbidden her to go into the saloon where those females of ill-repute plied their trade. The sound of music and laughter coming from one of the wooden canteens made her doubly anxious and lonesome.

'Can I purchase one of them melons?' she heard a gruff voice saying, and looked up into the dark eyes of a tall stranger. His black hair was thick and uncut, almost to his shoulders beneath his Stetson. He was bearded, slung with guns, and had the look of a prairie wanderer, but his weatherbeaten face had creased into a grin, and was not unfriendly.

'Sure, choose your own,' she said. 'Ten cents a big un, five cents a small un.'

'Kinda pricey, aincha?' Pete chose one and stabbed his Bowie into it, cutting himself a slice. He dug his teeth in with a loud sucking noise of pleasure. 'Man sure gits thirsty for a taste of fruit out in the mountains. Guess it's natural, ain't it?'

'What?'

'The craving,' His black eyes looked languorous as he gulped back the juice and eyed her slender form. 'Keeps the scurvy at bay.'

'I guess so.'

Pete cut himself another slice. 'Tell you what, I'm enjoying this so much and I've had a little win at the table so I'll give you a dollar. OK?'

The girl eyed him, uneasily, this not unhandsome stranger. There was a strong whiff of whiskey, and he looked a trifle unsteady. She hoped he wasn't going to bother her. She had enough troubles.

'Sure, thank you, suh. Take another.'

'Why you out marketing so late? Young gal like you should be dancing this time of night.'

'I'm waiting for my Pa. I don't know where he's gotten to. You say you're a gambling man, mistuh? You ain't seen an old fella? No, I guess you wouldn't have.'

'Grey hair? Straw sombrero? Five foot three? Suit two sizes too big for him? Boots caked with red mud? Guess he's a farmer.'

'That sounds like him. We got a few acres ten miles outa town.'

'Waal, he oughter stick to growin' melons. Dame Fortune ain't bin kind to him today. From what I heard he's lost everything. And here's me, who don't need it, won plenty.'

'Oh, Holy Mother help me,' the girl prayed, touching a silver crucifix at her throat. 'I told him. Oh, God!' And she began sobbing, silently, where she stood, barefoot in the dust.

Pete looked startled. Not another! If there was one thing he couldn't handle it was a sobbing woman. Awkwardly, he put an arm around her slim shoulders and pulled her to him, gently, patting her back. 'Hey, now, don't take on so.' He could feel her tears wetting his shirt.

The girl suddenly realized that she had her head buried in the stranger's chest, and there was something strong and comforting about his arms around her. She struggled away from him, mightily embarrassed. 'I'm sorry … what must you think of me.'

'Come on, now. Let's go over to that cantina and you can tell me what's wrong.'

'No.' She pulled away, making an effort to control herself. 'I don't go in places like that.'

'OK. Let's go find your Pa. What's the old rascal been up to?'

'Oh,' – she wiped her tears away on her sunbronzed arm, standing forlornly before him in her long, faded cotton dress, 'you ain't interested in our worries.'

'C'mon, kid. Howdja know? Give.'

'It's jest that since Ma died things have been going

bad. It hit Pa hard. Me, too. And then he gets behind with the feed bills, the payments on the loans. You know, everything.'

'I've run a ranch. I know the feeling.'

'Ours ain't a ranch. Jest a small place. But it's nice, fertile. Our own water. And then the man at the bank tells Pa that unless he comes up with two thousand dollars he's going to foreclose on the farm.'

'Two thousand?' Pete whistled. 'That's debts and everything?'

'Yes, and all he could raise was two hundred. We brought the wagon into town this morning. But I ain't seen him since.'

Pete tipped his hat over his eyes and scratched the back of his head. 'Sounds to me like he was trying to raise the two thousand at the faro table. Guess it was his last throw.'

'It ain't so bad,' she said, defiantly. 'We got the horse and the wagon. We can both work. We can head for Californee-yay. They say it's like paradise there. The peaches and oranges just grow themselves, and ... we can start again.'

'Mebbe you won't have to. What's your name?'

'Judy.'

'Waal, Judy, so happens I got two thousand dollars in my shirt. Mebbe I can make you a loan?'

'What?' She looked at him with astonishment.

'No. You jest show me where my Pa is. I ain't that kinda gal.'

'Come *on*.' Pete chuckled, because the two thousand wasn't exactly his in the first place. (In his somewhat intoxicated state the idea rather appealed to him of rearranging the balance of wealth, for Baxter hadn't honestly got the money in the first place, he'd taken it off such as Judy and her Pa). 'I wanna help ya!'

Judy shook her head and sat down on the melon pile. 'Jest wait 'til I put my boots on and you can show me where he is. That's all I need. And don't joke with me. It ain't kind.'

'You're a stubborn lil cuss, aincha?' Pete said, spitting out a melon pip and admiring her shapely leg. 'Jest look here, gal. I'm a lonesome cowboy. All I ask of you is that you're my partner tonight at thet dance hall yonder. I got a hankering to do the fandango. It's a long time since I swung a pretty gal on my arm. That's all.'

'You really got 2,000 dollars?' Judy looked up at him, doubtfully, wiping a blonde sprout of hair from out of her eyes. 'Well, mebbe I'll go to the dance with you. But that's all?'

'That's all. I may have shot down a few galoots in my time, but my intentions to you are honourable, young lady. In the morning we go to that bank and sort things out.'

'Hmm,' she mused, standing up. 'I don't know. Two thousand's a damn fortune. Where did you get it?'

'That,' he smiled, 'is my business. Howdja know I ain't some damn cattle baron?'

'You don't look like one.'

'OK, partners. I'll take a share in your farm. I wanna rest up my mare. I reckern Jesus has been misbehavin' hisself with her.'

Judy looked perplexed. 'Whadja mean, Jesus? You sure a funny fella. But, I dunno,' – she stuck out her hand, – 'I got the feelin' we can trust ya. Partners. Let's go tell Pa.'

Pete shook her hand, swung her around and tucked it in under his arm. 'Tell you what, we'll buy your old man a couple of enchiladas and a beer. I seen a nice hotel where he can git some shut-eye. Or he can sit all night and watch those other damn fools lose all their money.'

There was a spring in the girl's step as she walked with him across the square. Pete suddenly let rip a rebel yell, giving her a whirl, practising the steps for the fandango. Judy laughed with a mixture of relief and excitement. He sure was a crazy sort of character. She didn't know whether he was telling the truth or cruelly teasing her. But she let him take her hand and lead her.

Her father was still lying on the sidewalk, staring into space, a look of despair creasing his features. Judy roused him.

'Hey, Pa. This here's Pete. He seems a real friendly fella. He wants to take me dancing. He says in the morning he'll pay off what we owe on the farm. Two thousand dollars, Pa.'

'Don't be stupid, gal,' – her father looked at her with horror, and up at the gunman, – 'you don't believe that, do you? I'm finished, gal. Thet's all there is to it.'

'He says we'll be partners if we look after his horse. He won't give you the cash tonight because he reckons you'd be tempted to spend it in thet durn gambling hell.'

'No, Judy.' He waved Pete's outstretched hand away. 'I ain't being bribed by the devil. I know what this man wants. So do you gal. You ain't going to sacrifice yourself on my account for a few dollars. I brought you up right, gal. I ain't puttin' you on the road to perdition.'

'Aw, c'mon, Paw. I only goin' dancing. I want to. I ain't never been nowhere before. It ain't like you think. Mistuh Pete here's a real gennlman.'

'Waal,' Pete grinned, 'I wouldn't rely on it. Us Texans are quick on the draw. No, ahm only joshing. She'll be safe with me. You'll have her back in the morning.'

'Come on, Pa.' She helped him up and they took him along to the hotel, gave him food and drink and bedded him down. 'You'll feel better in the morning.'

Pete stuck out his hand. 'I got a stallion someplace.

Mebbe I could go half-shares in thet farm of yourn? Start a breedin' ranch? We gotta talk it over. Looks like they need some new blood around hyar.'

This time her father accepted the proffered handshake. A gleam had come back into his faded blue eyes. 'If you put it like that. Tom Vine. Thet's the handle. You go along now, enjoy yourselves. You take care of her, you hear?'

Mr Vine was left looking at the twenty dollar gold piece in his palm. He drank his beer, pensively, and out of the window watched his daughter walk off, her arm around the waist of the lanky Texan. He didn't like it. This fellow didn't act like no ordinary guide or cow puncher. He'd got some kinda past. Any fool could see that. But, he'd acted handsome so far. Judy was a good girl. He believed, he hoped, she could look after herself.

On a bend of the track from Red Rock to Connor's Crossing there was a water tower and log pile. The wood was cut from the mountain-side and hewed in readiness for stoking the locomotive's furnace by a man who lived in a little cabin alongside. He was standing there in his faded long johns, axe in hand and started, involuntarily, when he saw a powerfully-built man, of dark and ugly looks, riding towards him. His first thought was to go for his shotgun. He decided this might not be a good idea. He knew this man had the power of life or death over him. Everything about him seemed to speak of that, from the coat of ratskins, their naked tails hanging down, to his wide leather chaps, which were decorated with straggly scalps. The bounty hunter liked to boast that they represented near every tribe on the mid-continent. Even his saddle horn was behatted with the pubic part of some poor squaw. He had a carbine strapped across his back, long-barrelled .45s on his hips, and two ropes of bullets across his shoulders. He was astride a big black stallion that stood shuddering and snorting, wide-eyed. There was foam at its mouth, and it was flecked with spittle, running with sweat, its sides bleeding from spur rowels. The stallion had once answered to the name of Jesus. The bounty hunter had taken him from an Indian who had shot his own horse from under him. He had killed the Indian, cut his head off with a machete and put it in a sack.

'You seen a tall Texan ride through on a grey?'

'Sure. Yes'day marnin', headed fer the Crossin'. What's goin' arn? Ain't bin a train through fer days. Telegraph wire's gawn dead.'

'Trouble. The bridge is down. Ah got one of the bastards hyar.'

The bounty hunter's fierce eyes burned redly in his bearded face as he hoisted a gunny sack that hung from the saddle. A flock of flies were droning noisily upon it. It slowly dripped blood. The hayseed knew a human head was inside. The man spat in the dust and spurred the stallion on, on along the track.

THIRTEEN

The sound of a bailee, as they called their shindigs, lured Pete and the girl towards a long wooden canteen of new planed planks where the Irish were holding forth. It was no great shakes as a ballroom, benches and tables along the walls lit by candles in tin sconces or stuck in bottles, but it was packed with humanity, mainly the bridge-builders and some of their ladies. Their attire might not have been of the finest – rough woollen dresses, the men in muddy, concertina-like suits, mufflers at their throats – but it was Friday night and they planned to have a good time. Their music swirled through the night, a savage wild mixture of squeeze box, bull fiddle, weird Irish bagpipes and a muffled, throbbing, Indian drum. The songs given voice were either liltingly full of melancholy, or wild and pounding ones of rebel misdeeds. Sometimes a big raucous-voiced man called Cripple Creek Jack got up and roared about the mines or the railroad:

'We work all day and we work all night – we live on powder and dynamite.'

And a favourite chorus which everybody joined in:

'...and leave a little in the bottle for the morning!'

The dancing was unrestrained, a lot of toe-tapping and heel-kicking, and shimmying back and forth, the rounds called off by Cripple Creek Jack: 'Balance yer pardners and all hands round. ...'

Pete reluctantly gave up his gunbelt and rifle at the door, grabbed hold of Judy's hand, and put an arm around her waist, swinging her into the throng. And they were jogging and whooping and waltzing with the rest of them. If he paused to grab a swig of his new bottle of Knock 'Em Dead, Judy quickly pulled him back into the dance again.

Finally, even she had to beg for a rest, and, flushed and elated, she leaned against the wall and watched Pete, whose eyes were going a trifle glassy.

'Whoo-whee!' he whistled. 'What the hail. I'm past caring. Ain't had so much fun in a long time.'

It was well gone midnight when he staggered out into the night air. He went tacking across the main drag, his knees gone to water, and the girl had to put an arm around his waist to support him. It was not an unusual sight at that time of night, so nobody took much notice. Somehow he made it to the stable door, and, swaying there, he put a hand around her slender neck and kissed her. 'Lips like nectar,' he breathed.

'That's more than I can say about yourn,' Judy said, clinging to him. 'Ole whiskey breath. You sure have had a skinful.'

'I sure hev,' Pete chuckled as the ground came up to thud him. He lay on his back, looking up at a coruscating expanse of stars, helpless. Before it all blacked out on him.

'Men!' Judy exploded.

FOURTEEN

Judy was asleep in the hay of the stable when Pete awoke in the morning, sunlight squinting through the beams. She looked as innocent as a child lying there. What had happened? A pang of guilt struck him. A sense of retribution about to fall. His sixth sense told him that the fates were closing in. Or maybe it was just a hangover. He began to pull his boots on. He couldn't remember even taking them off. Judy stirred, her flower-blue eyes opening, focusing on him.

'Hello,' she smiled.

'What happened?' Pete mumbled. 'I mean last night.'

'What happened?' she sighed, stretching her arms back. 'It was wonderful.'

'It was?'

'All that dancing.'

'I mean ... uh ... after that.'

'Oh, you! Don't tell me you don't remember ...'

'Waal ... uh ... no.'

'You passed out. You snored. Drunk as a pig. I had to git a passin' feller to help haul you in here.'

'It's true what they say about that stuff, then? You won't git further than fifty yards. I was just testin'. Knock 'Em Dead, they call it. You all right?'

'Sure, I'm all right.' She sneezed as a piece of straw got

up her nose. The horses rustled and stamped, and she rolled over and looked up at him. 'I feel heavenly. Mind you, a mite disappointed. That was some kiss you give me.'

'C'mon, kid, I'm old enough to be your uncle. I promised your Paw, too. Think yourself lucky. Many a gal's been ruined by a feller like me.'

'You ain't that old, Pete.' She nibbled at a straw, studying him, thoughtfully. 'Are you really going to go into partnership with me and Pa?'

Pete's hand went to inside his shirt as he remembered the wad of 2,000 dollars. He eased it out and showed it to her. 'Lucky that was an honest feller who hauled me in there.'

'Mercy! Can I hold it? I never seen so much in my life.'

He watched her flick through the dollars. She looked like an excited child at birthday time. She blew upwards to try to flick a long blonde strand of hair from out of her eyes. And, as she saw him try to get himself together, she threw her slim arms around his neck and whispered, 'Don't go, yet.'

He laid her gently back in the straw and his dark eyes brooded on her blues ones for a long time. He gave her a kiss, but it was more a kiss of affection than of lust.

'How old are you, seventeen?'

'Old enough,' she said. 'Mebbe it's time I learned about love. You look like a good teacher to me.'

'Nope,' he said, and sat up before he changed his mind. 'Jest 'cause I'm givin' you an' your ole man this cash you don't hev to do that.'

'It's not that,' Judy whispered, insistently. 'Don't you understand, Pete? I want to.'

'Holy Moses,' he mumbled, like an embarrassed cowpoke. 'Never thought I'd turn down such a pretty lil chickadee. That's the way it's gotta be. I feel kinda protective towards you. We don't want there to be two instead of one of you, do we? At least not yetaways.'

'What do you mean?'

'I mean leavin' this town different to how you arrived. I mean, doin' those sort of things a gal's liable to have a baby. An' iffen your ole man kicked his boots you'd be on your own and unmarried and that's the surest way to the pathway of perdition.'

'You think I'd end up like one of them casino gals? But, why? I'd have you, Pete. We could be married.'

'Hey, hey, steady on now, honey. You're sweet and lovely and I'm not saying I wouldn't like to roll you in this hay. I sure have got a hankerin' to settle down, and you sure look like you'd make a nice lil missus. And I ain't sayin' I wouldn't have last night if I'd been able. But this mornin' I got more horse sense. I gotta leave things awhile, see how the land lies. Mebbe I can stay, mebbe I can't. You sure got me all confused.'

Judy lay and looked at him, puzzled. She wasn't offering herself because of the money, because he was going to help them. He sure was a strange character to think that. She suddenly felt rejected and cheapened. 'I like you,' she implored. 'I cain't help it.'

'I like you, too,' he said. 'That's why I ain't goin' to. C'mon, kid. A dip in thet horse trough and a strong black cawfee. Thet's what we need.'

Mr Vine wasn't at the hotel, but they knew where he would be: at the tables. He had been there all night.

'You wouldn't believe it. Your twenty took me up to 500 dollars. Now I'm back to twenty again.'

'You gotta give up this gamblin',' Pete said. 'It ain't good for the heart. I'm gonna put 2,000 dollars into the farm. We'll go across and sort it out with the bank. You and I, we goin' t'be pardners, Mr Vine.'

'Jeez. I don't know how to thank you, Pete.' They wandered over to the bank together.

FIFTEEN

Jim Robinson was a tall man, raw-boned and angular, his slab of crow-black hair and bristling beard giving him an appearance not unlike Pete's in many ways. He, too, was garbed Western-style, in a stetson, bandanna, leather chaps, boots and spurs. But there the similarity ceased. He was crude and vindictive and greedy for land. He would do anybody down to get his hand on more of it. His father had been a famed frontiersman before the War and given his name to Robinson's Landing, which was on a lakeside ten miles further along through the mountains, the way the railroad was heading. He had inherited his father's rights to run a trading post there and had sold some of his land to Mr Vine. He had given him a mortgage, and encouraged him to buy goods, plough-share, wagon, seed and so forth, at high interest rates. Now he had taken to running the bank at Connor's Crossing one day a week and had become a crony of John Chiltern, the rail boss.

'Two thousand dollars in debts seems a hell of a lot to me,' Pete said, as they spoke to Robinson in his bank. 'I'd like to take a squint at Mr Vine's accounts.'

'What's it got to do with you?'

'We might be going into partnership.'

Robinson was visibly irritated as he got the accounts out of the safe. 'I ain't got time to mess around. I got

business to do. Thar 'tis, in black and white. Everythin'
ahm owed writ down. That's the interest. I don't
suppose you'd understand it.'

'I bought the stuff fair and square,' Mr Vine said. 'But
I thought the interest was goin' t'be thirty per cent a year,
not a week.'

'Thet's what we agreed. You ain' in Sain' Looey now,
you know.'

'These figures don't make much sense to me,' Pete
said, scratching his beard. 'Ah reckern you bin robbin'
him blind.'

'Say what you like.' Robinson said. 'You cain't prove
nuthin'. Law's on my side.'

'Is it? Yeh, it usually is, ain't it? Waal, OK, you win,' –
he slapped the 2,000 dollars down, – 'ahm payin' off this
debt.'

Robinson snapped the books shut, waved the cash
away. 'Too late, hombre. Vine here had notice that I was
goin' to foreclose yesterday unless the money was
forthcomin'. That was the deadline. That land now
reverts to my property.'

'And I say it don't.' Pete's hands caught Robinson by
his shirt neck, and, in spite of his weight, hauled him
halfway across the desk. He scowled in Robinson's face.
'You hand over them damn deeds, pronto, signed, with
a proper receipt, you cheatin' bastard. Or mebbe I'll be
callin' in a lawyer friend of mine from Kansas City to
take a look at your affairs. Unless I save myself the
bother. Savvy?'

Robinson's face flushed with anger, but he backed
down. 'OK,' he said, 'ahm gonna overlook the deadline
this time. But I don' think Mistuh Chiltern's gonna be
too happy about this.'

Pete grinned at Mr Vine, letting his grip relax.
'Mebbe. Mebbe not. You got your farm back, Tom.'

SIXTEEN

To celebrate, they loaded the Vines' wagon with supplies.

'You gotta come out take a look at the place. It ain't much, but it sure is half yourn now.'

First Pete guided Judy into a seamstress's shop. Her long blue dress was looking awful faded by the sun and farmwork. 'Got anythung colourful to fit this young lady?'

The seamstress had taken to stocking some glitzy dresses to satisfy the tastes of the fallen angels over at the casino. Judy chose a neat little number of vividly-striped Indian silk that clung to her slim waist, with plenty of swirl for dancing.

'How about some of these lovely white stockings to go with it?' the seamstress suggested, pulling them out. 'Arrived only last week from the East.'

'Sure, sling 'em in,' Pete said. 'Anything else?'

'Wow,' Judy cried, thrilled, as they came out into the sun. 'I'm going to look sassier than any of them ladies at the fandango. Can't we go dancing again, Pete? I'd love to.'

'Mebbe,' he said.

He was glad that nothing heavy had occurred between them. It was funny, he had had no such reservations with Katherine Baxter, and she was only a few years older than the girl. But, then, she was a proud, haughty bitch who had asked for her come-uppance. He tried to imagine where she was, how she was dressed, in her starched lace blouses, bustles and jewellery, but the only image that came into his mind was of her naked in that mountain pool, her body smooth and slippery and shiny against his. ...

'Who's that?' Judy cried, fear in her voice, snapping Pete out of his reverie.

A horseman was cantering across the ground towards them, a big man, a sack dangling from his pommel around which a horde of flies buzzed. Their noise was audible. His face was grim and he was dressed in a ratskin coat and a black high-crowned hat. His boots were stained with blood. Pete froze when he saw him and pushed the girl away from him.

The Indian Killer drew in his horse fifty paces from him. It was a powerful black stallion that had been treated mighty bad. Pete realized, with a start, that it was his horse, christened Jesus Christ by the Jew Elie Strauss. He had left it with Howling Wolf, and, seeing it, he feared the worst.

Jesus had recognized Pete too, pricking up his ears and whinnying, plaintively, but the bounty hunter curbed his bit, savagely. The man's red-rimmed eyes were on Pete so fixedly that it made him feel the morning had gone cold. There was something unearthly about this man.

'Pete Bowen,' The Killer shouted. 'I bin looking for you. You thought you could shake me off your trail but you thought wrong.'

And he tossed the bloody sack towards Pete, rolling across the dust. It came to rest in a cloud of pursuing flies.

'It's your friend,' he said. 'The Injun. I took his head first. Now I'm gonna take yourn.'

'Over my dead body,' Pete muttered, before realizing that the words were not very wise.

He saw The Indian Killer's hand move, a pearl-handled Colt Frontier seemingly leap into it, and with his right hand he went for his own gun. As he loosed the first slug off a scalding pain, severing one of his fingers, sent the revolver flying.

For seconds he was held, sickened by the pain and the sight of his finger in the dust. And, in those moments, frightened by the explosion, the stallion reared. Or, perhaps he had some idea of helping his former master? Whatever, The Killer missed with his second shot.

Pete reached crosshand and pulled out his left-hand Smith and Wesson as The Killer hauled the stallion around, rowelling his Mexican spurs into his flanks, forcing the horse forward onto his opponent. Pete tried to aim the .44, but with the horse on top of him, his jaws slavering at the bit, he couldn't get a correct bead, and with the pain juicing through him all he could think was, 'Oh, shee-it!' as the shot went wide and his own horse trampled him to the ground.

The stallion was whinnying and kicking, resisting the spurs and bit furiously, and The Killer laughed and forced him to swirl back towards the fallen man, standing in the stirrups over him, pointing the big Colt Frontier at his head. Pete looked up and it was like looking into the face of a filthy snarling pariah dog.

Suddenly the bounty hunter was pitched from his saddle riddled with buckshot as an explosion echoed. It was from a shotgun held by Tom Vine. He walked across from his wagon and emptied the second barrel into the gunman's heart.

'Whew!' Pete said, as Judy ran across and helped him

to his feet. 'I thought my time had come.'

They stood staring at the dead man as townspeople ran up, and three armed railway guards arrived.

'Arrest these men,' snapped one of them. 'I've had enough of desperadoes taking the law into their own hands.'

SEVENTEEN

Pete could not hold back his gasps of pain as Cripple Creek Jack probed at the raw stump of his finger with a needle. His teeth bit deep into the bullet as the needle probed his nerve ends. Again. And again. And again. He could not prevent unmanly tears spurting into his eyes. He had refused laudanum, but was beginning to wish he hadn't. He had, however, seen too many men in the Civil War, tens of thousands of them there must have been, become dependent on the drug. It was one thing having a touch of bottle fever, but another being a lousy raving drug addict. 'Aargh!' The needle went in again. Somehow Jack finally got the stump stitched up and the blood flow staunched and bandaged.

'Mighty grateful!' Pete breathed a sigh of relief that for the moment it was over. 'Guess I'm lucky you know about doctoring.'

'We cain't let you bleed to death afore we hang you.' One of the railroad guards gave a hollow laugh. 'Mr Chiltern should be back soon. He's been out up front a few days surveyin' the route. He'll be mighty surprised to hear what's bin happenin'. I don't think much of your chances.'

They had him held, his legs in irons, in a sturdy back room of the store. It looked like he had escaped the bounty killer to end on the gallows.

'Serves me right,' he mumbled, 'fer hanging around. All thet whuskey last night musta slowed my reactions. Poor ole Howling. Mighta known. Guess I shoulda gotten outa here.'

John Chiltern was not pleased when he got back from a week's expedition with a party of surveyors, blasters, and railroad engineers: the bridge at Twin Peaks blown, the train robbed, six of Mr Baxter's men killed, and his fiancée kidnapped. And, who knew what she had suffered at the hands of those bandits? Two riders had just got through to say that she was safe and well, and that the man who had been shotgunned was Mr Baxter's bounty hunter. He had hunted his last bounty.

The first thing to do was to get a gang organized and a train steaming back to the Twin Peaks chasm to start rebuilding work immediately. Jim Robinson had then bothered him with a tale of being forced and threatened by some mysterious wanderer to give the old man Vine his title back. That land was essential to the progress of the railroad. Chiltern had massive funds available, but he had no intention of paying these peasant farmers more than peanuts. Who did this gunman think he was?

'You damn fool,' he shouted at Robinson. 'Am I surrounded by half-wits?'

Chiltern was a tall, robust, ruddy-cheeked man, older than Katherine by some twenty years. He was used to getting his way with men, of not suffering fools gladly. Like Baxter he did not like to make his money by blatantly breaking the law. There were ways of stepping around it. Although he could be harsh and tough towards his men, when he was in Katherine's company he became tongue-tied and awkward, overawed by the haughty beauty of the young woman. He found it difficult to do more than touch her hand, her waist, but he wanted her, desperately. And, there was also the fact that she, her youth and culture, her father's money and property, would be a good investment. The news of her kidnap had unnerved him, made him feel jittery.

He was tempted to have these two suspects hanged on the spot. It would solve the problem of Vine's land. And he was pretty certain this man must be the desperado responsible. But he was always wary. If word got out about summary executions, or about the money he and Baxter had been making – the newspapers used ugly words like 'swindling smalltime homesteaders' – there could be a commission of enquiry. And, who knew, loss of the contract?

Chiltern didn't waste much time with Tom Vine. He was transparently honest. Vine said he thought his newfound partner was being attacked by a bandit and had gone in and helped him. In these parts it was unlikely any jury would convict him. The man suspected of being Black Pete Bowen was a different kettle of fish. If he had touched Katherine ... Chiltern was angry enough to kill him, personally.

EIGHTEEN

Katherine Baxter had thought long and hard before swearing out a complaint against the man, believed to be the outlaw Black Pete Bowen, of kidnapping, bodily harm, robbery of her cash and jewellery and rape. It was the latter charge that worried her most. Not something a respectable young lady of fashion cared to have her name linked to. But, on the other hand, it was probably best to let her husband-to-be, John Chiltern, know that she was not a virgin as there was always the possibility that her wild, mad intercourse that night might have made her pregnant. If so, she would need to be able to explain how that had occurred. So rape it had to be.

She was in her bedroom of the large wooden ranch house on the edge of Red Rock, which, although a goodly way from civilization, was furnished with all the comforts money could buy – crystal chandeliers, velvet curtains, a nicely-covered chaise longue, polished tables, vases, ornaments and soft carpets. She was vigorously brushing her thick tresses of hair that crackled and sparkled like red gold in the setting sun slanting through the window. She was sat in her cotton and lace underthings preparing to go down to dinner. She wondered, sometimes, how her mother could have run off from all this gracious living, never to return. And she recalled her own strange plea to the outlaw that night to take her with him. Did she have the same bad streak as her mother? It was crazy. She, Katherine, needed the luxuriousness of these surroundings, needed a man like John Chiltern, his responsibility and riches. And yet, a germ of dissatisfaction, of restlessness, crept inside her. She tried not to think of that night, but it was always there.

There was a tap on the door and her father's voice and she called out to him to enter.

'Hello, honey, how you feeling?'

'Fine. Much better.'

'They've got the telegraph line fixed up again. They're holding a man down at Connor's Crossing. John wants you to go down and identify him for the trial.'

'He does?' She was startled. 'How can I do that? The bridge is. ...'

'They've got it temporarily fixed. We could take a train to one side and walk across. Catch another car the other side. It's not as bad as they thought. The basic supports are still sound.'

'Can't they bring him back here?'

'Sure, they could do. But the man they've got denies having anything to do with it. John's got a lot on his plate down there. If they could get a positive identification from you? It might be best to give John your support. Talk things over with him. The sooner you two get married the better it will be.'

'Yes,' she said, and gave her father a smile of understanding. 'Of course.'

'Good. We'll go down in the morning.'

John Chiltern liked to sport shiny knee-high English riding boots, jodhpurs, a hacking jacket and checked waistcoat. He liked to cut a dash before the men, to let them know his was a world apart. Of course, he too carried a six-shooter in a buttoned leather holster on his belt and wore a low-crowned Western Stetson.

He had decided to interview the prisoner a second time and get tough, if necessary. This sort of rogue needed softening up. 'You are still sticking to your ludicrous story? You say your name's Pete Johnson, you're a guide and professional hunter?'

'That's true,' Pete drawled. 'One of the Johnsons, of Independence, family of honest horse dealers in Missouri.'

'I can't say I ever met an *honest* horse dealer before,' Chiltern snapped, and his men laughed.

'We're known for plain dealin',' Pete said. 'Thassall. In fact I got a receipt in my pocket for that black stallion that bastard was ridin'. Bought it for seventy dollars from Eli Strauss at Silverillo Colorado, this winter past. That evil horse-thievin' bushwhacker jumped me 300 miles back in Indian Territory. I bin trailin him ever since. When I caught up and challenged him about the theft he turned his guns on me, as you know.' Pete fumbled in his shirt pocket left-handed for the receipt. His right was still far too painful to use. 'There. There's Eli's signature and there's the brand. You can check it out. That stallion belongs to me.'

John Chiltern took the crumpled receipt and nodded. 'This at least seems to be in order. What I want to know is where you got the two thousand dollars from to give to Tom Vine?'

'Them's my life savings. Don't believe in banks.'

'So, why give them to Vine?'

'Why? Waal, I felt kinda sorry for him the way you railroad people trying to run him off his land. I needed to rest up my horse to foal. And, to tell you the truth, I gotta admit I've taken a fancy to that purty lil gal of his.'

'Truth? I don't believe a word of it!' John Chiltern crashed his riding crop down on Pete's severed stub. 'The truth is what I want.'

A half-choked-back scream came from Pete as the bare nerves seared with fire. He pulled his hand back, a retch of agony on his face.

'That money was the ransom money paid to you for the release of Katherine Baxter, isn't that so?' And Chiltern slashed his crop at the finger once more. 'Isn't it, Bowen? You were the gunman on the train.'

'My name's Pete Johnson,' he muttered, as a blow from one of the men caught him in the solar plexus and doubled him up. His black eyes glimmered as he met Chiltern's. He shielded his finger and gritted out, 'One day you're going to regret doin' this.'

Katherine and her father reached Connor's Crossing at midnight. They put up at the hotel and in the morning John Chiltern took them to see the prisoner. In the 'softening up' his men had been careful not to hit his face. 'I can't get anything out of him. Are you sure you're ready for this, Katherine?'

'I want to see the despicable rat brought to justice, that's all,' she said, as they unlocked the back room. 'After the way he treated me.'

Pete was huddled up on the dirt floor and groaned as one of the guards poked him with his boot. 'Git on your feet, hombre,' the guard said, hauling him up. 'There's a lady present.'

In spite of his aching ribs Pete raised a bloody finger stub towards his hat and mumbled, 'Howdy, miss. Or is it ma'am?'

Katherine studied him for moments and said, 'This isn't the man.'

'What do you mean?' Chiltern burst out. 'Are you

sure?'

'I spent days being hauled about a mountain-side with a noose around my neck, beaten and humiliated and ... surely I would recognize him, wouldn't I?'

'All right dear. Don't get distraught. Sit down over there.' Chiltern patted her shoulder and turned to Baxter. 'This is all very unfortunate.'

'It durn sure is,' Pete muttered.

In an undertone Chiltern asked Baxter, 'Can anybody else identify him?'

'The man was at the station, but he was standing back in the shadow. I hardly noticed him. I couldn't be sure. And Mr Mirick says he was wearing a heavy bandanna mask when he robbed the train and it could have been anybody the same height. The men who saw him in the saloon are all dead. In the shoot-out he was in the distance most the time. It's all very odd. A pity I didn't mark those notes. Katherine's very upset but she wouldn't lie.'

'Wouldn't she?' Chiltern said. 'Maybe she doesn't want to go through with the trial? Maybe more than she's saying happened up in those mountains?'

'Now then, John, you're getting upset, too. No cause to think things like that,' Baxter whispered. 'I tell you what, young Davey's outside. Brought him along to carry the bags. He twice spoke to the kidnapper.'

'Bring him in,' Chiltern snapped.

'Are you saying you don't believe me?' Katherine was bridling up, imperious, but panicky, as Davey was ushered in. 'If I say I haven't met this man before, I haven't, that's all.'

Davey eyed her, and Black Pete, craftily. He looked at Baxter and remembered the cuts across his face he had given him with his whip. 'What's going on?' he said.

'Come on, Davey,' Chiltern roared. 'Is this the man

you gave the money to? And remember, I want the truth.'

A smile flickered on Davey's lips as he glanced first at Katherine and then at Pete. 'No. I nevuh seen this feller before today.'

'Perhaps now you'll believe me,' Katherine said, and rushed out of the room, her silk dress rustling.

The men stood looking dismayed for some while as the guards unlocked Pete's leg irons.

'What about my black stallion?'

Chiltern thrust the receipt at him. 'Take it. And get out of this township. And keep moving. And tell the Vines if they've any sense, to keep moving with you because they're not going to be able to hang onto that land. I don't want to see any of your faces around these parts again. Understand?'

'Sure,' Pete said, soothingly. 'What about my guns?'

'Give them to him. And see him off the premises.'

'Waal,' Pete thought he might as well say 'at least that dog got what he deserved. Carrying people's heads around like that. The feller was insane. I won't be stayin' for his funeral.'

NINETEEN

Mr Vine and Judy were waiting for him as he came out.

'Are you all right?' Judy cried. 'I bin so worried.'

'They mighta beat me but they didn' manage to hang me. I'm free,' he said, looking up at the blue sky and filling his lungs with air. 'Thet's what counts, ain't it?'

They had their wagon with the grey mare hitched to the back. 'You gonna come look at the farm? It's half yourn now,' Mr Vine said.

'I gotta thank you for your intervention, suh. Guess you saved my hide. That feller beat me to the draw fair and square. I'm gittin' too old fer gun-fightin'. Or mebbe all thet whusky and dancin' the other night slowed me down.'

'You saved my bacon so we're quits, ain't we? How's the finger?'

'Waal, thet durn Cripple Creek Jack kinda creased my nerves with his probing. And Chiltern didn't help none. You could call it torture. Still, nuthin' that a little rest and recreation won't cure.' He looked, ruefully, at the bandaged gap where the second finger of his right hand used to be. 'That was my courtin' finger!'

'Lucky it weren't your trigger finger,' Mr Vine said.

'Yeah, I reckern I'm gonna be needin' that.'

They walked across to the stables to collect Jesus. The

livery had given him a feed and washed him down. Pete examined the rowellings on his side. Like him, with a little rest he would be as good as new. In spite of his condition the stallion looked eager and glad to see Pete and was soon nuzzling at his shirt.

'He's your horse, sure enough,' the livery ostler said. 'He's been whinnying and kicking up somethung awful while you bin in the pokey.'

'He's telepathic,' Pete said, as he took him out and tied him alongside the grey. 'He musta guessed they were beating the daylights outa me.'

'C'mon, let's git,' Mr Vine said, shaking the reins. And the three of them sat upfront as the wagon rolled out of Connor's Crossing. The gunmen, shotguns hooked under their arms, watched them go, ominously.

Katherine was on the veranda of the hotel with her father and John Chiltern taking coffee. She pretended not to notice Pete, and the young girl by his side, as they passed. But she could not help wondering where they were going to.

'I only met that lousy bounty hunter a couple of times,' Mr Baxter laughed. 'I must agree his personal hygiene was somewhat lacking, even for these parts. His sartorial sense even worse. Scalps and ratskins. And his approach to the Indian problem – kill 'em all – is becoming outmoded. I reckon we've got to be a little more enlightened.'

'Well,' Chiltern said, his face stern. 'At least he got that one who abducted Katherine.'

And so they ambled merrily along on the wagon through the pines that bordered the bubbling muddy river until they reached Lost Lake and Robinson's Landing. Jim Robinson stood in his store doorway and watched them, surly and hangdog, a revolver in his belt.

Mr Vine ya-hooed and waved his deeds to his land at him, and they climbed on up along the valley, the natural way the railroad would come, until they reached their farm at Lodgepole Creek, which lay in its way between two steep rock escarpments.

'It ain't much but it's home,' Mr Vine said.

And, looking at it, Pete had to silently agree. The ground was harsh and unfriendly, except where Mr Vine had managed to dam it and irrigate it, and squash and sweet corn and other vegetables were growing in the red mud. The house was even worse, a ramshackle edifice made of bits and pieces of rock and stones, its thatched pine roof propped up on rickety lodgepoles. The barn and outhouses weren't much better.

Judy proudly showed him the living area and two sparsely partitioned bedrooms in which the furniture mainly consisted of wooden crates laid with Indian blankets. There was an elk skin covering the raised stone floor, its antlers propped against the wall.

'We gotta fix the roof one of these days,' Mr Vine said. 'That's our main problem. Don't keep out cloudbursts. And you git rats and snakes in the thatch. Fortunately, the snakes eat the rats.'

'Thet ain't countin' the skunks thet git underneath,' Judy said. 'We got plenty of them round these parts.'

Pete corralled the horses and mule and Judy milked the goats while her Pa rattled buckets to feed the hogs.

'Everything's a bit tumbledown, but nuthin' a few nails won't fix,' Mr Vine said, as they sat at dinner and Judy smiled across at Pete. 'We sure could do with a young fella around here to help with the work.'

A frown flickered over Pete's face as he pushed his cleared plate away and lit a cheroot. 'I surely would like to stay,' he said. 'I'm tired of wandering. But, I gotta tell ya the truth. That money I gave ya wasn't honestly come by. Them fellas have suspicioned me, but they cain't prove it. Yet. One of these days mebbe they'll figure it out. I got a list of offences as long as my arm they're after me for in five states. I kinda hoped I'd got far enough away, but I allus end up doin' some durn fool thung. I got a price on my head and they ain't gonna let me fergit.'

'Waal, I kinda suspicioned ya, too. I mean what would you wanna go givin' me thet much money for if it were yourn? But, what the heck, we ain't complainin'. Myself, I've lived honest all my life, but now and again a man has to turn a blind eye.'

'Sure, old-timer, mebbe. But Chiltern and his men ain't goin' to. They warned me to git movin' and to keep movin' and suggested it would be healthy if you moved on, too. This thung ain't finished yet. Mebbe it would be wise to take their advice 'fore there's more bloodshed.'

'I ain't moving,' Mr Vine spluttered. 'You can move on your way, Pete. And mebbe take my gal Judy with you. But I'm sticking. This is my land.'

'In that case, I guess I'd better hang around.'

TWENTY

Some days passed and Pete occupied himself mending a few fences, hoeing the rows of beans. Like most Westerners he was more interested in taking a hammer and knocking around among the rocks. But there didn't seem to be anything that might interest an assayer. Just a few streaks of quartz on the cliff wall. The bruises they had inflicted on his body with their boots and fists began to soak out of him, gradually, and he could turn in his sleep in the night without groaning with pain. Even the constant throbbing, thrumming nerve-end edginess of his severed finger began to muffle, like Indian drums, and when he took the bloody bandage away he was relieved to see the absence of gangrene. It was even beginning to heal. Judy carefully cut the stitches out, while Pete bit on the bullet again. It didn't do his teeth much good.

'I wonder what happened to Howling Wolf's head?' The thought occurred to Pete one night as they sat at supper. 'I reckon them town curs at Connor's Crossing must have golloped it up. Along with my finger top.'

Judy squealed with laughter. 'What a thing to say when we're eating! Who was Howling Wolf, Pete?'

'He was my *compadre*. A Wichita. A very strange Indian. We rode together. They took him away and educated him back east. He's full of crazy ideas about ancient Greece. He even reckons classical Greek had the same syntax and similar alphabet to Cherokee, the Iroquoian dialect. Or so he says. He's talking about bringing out a Cherokee newspaper. I cain't see many Indians buying it!'

'You're talking about him as if he's alive. Surely, that was his head? He's dead.'

'Yeah,' Pete said. 'Guess I cain't really believe it yet. Knew him a while. Got kinda fond of him. He was a nice kid. Even though he tried to kill me once. Threw a knife at me. Understandable. Poor ole Henry. You'd a liked him. I never realized before him that Injins had such a good sense of humour. He came back West, thought he could re-learn all the Indian ways. We used to laugh about it. He just wasn't going to make it as a warrior.'

'He sounds nice.'

'He was.'

'But,' the realization suddenly came to her, 'if that was his head, then it must have been you and him?'

'That robbed the train? I would forget that deduction, Judy. Forget what I said. I should never have gotten him into it.'

Judy couldn't leave it there. 'That woman. It was you. You kidnapped and raped her, both of you.'

'Nope, not Henry.'

'You?'

'Waal, let's say she wasn't exactly unwilling.'

'You're going to see her again, aincha?' Judy cried, as, later that evening, she watched him grease his bullets, spin the cylinders of his .44's, stuff them, butts forward, into their holsters. 'You're crazy. They'll kill you.'

He washed his body under the pump, combed back his long hair, put on a clean wool shirt and grinned at the girl. 'The night was meant for roving. Who was it said that? Some poet.' He slung his Texan saddle over Jesus, who danced, his black coat shimmering over powerful elastic muscles, eager to be away. 'And the moon'll show us the way.'

She ran and grabbed his arm. 'Don't go, Pete. I couldn't bear it if anything happened to you.'

'C'mon, Judy. I'll be back.'

'What's so special about ... about *her*?'

'I dunno. It's like the tides that rule the oceans. I jest gotta see her again. C'mon, kid, I told you I ain't the man for you.'

Judy bit her lip as she watched him swing into the saddle and ride away into the darkness of the trees. 'Serve me right,' she said, 'fer gittin' mixed up with a no-good outlaw.'

The stallion galloped like the wind along the shore of Lost Lake, his master going with him hanging low over his neck, urging him on, his mane flaying in his eyes, leaping fallen trees, turning to climb up a steep bluff to bypass the lights of Robinson's Landing and on along the trail through the dark pines. Man and horse seemingly as one, a fine rapture and excitement running through him to be flying through the night, at the prospect of encroaching danger.

He tied the stallion in a stand of trees, and approached Connor's Crossing on foot. From the scraping of fiddles it sounded like the railroad labourers were having another bailie. Others were sat around their smoky campfires. He could hear giggles and screams of laughter coming from the long log cabin where the gambling went on. Moving on around the backs of the clapboard buildings he could see a couple of late diners sat in the restaurant of the hotel. It was

Baxter and Chiltern. Katherine was not with them. Had she already retired to bed? There were lights on in various bedrooms. Which one, he wondered, was hers? As he stood in the shadows looking up he felt as if he wanted to howl like a lonesome frustrated coyote. Suddenly he saw her at a window, her long red braids hanging loose, her hour-glass body silhouetted in a diaphanous negligee. She drew the curtains together and was gone. Pete's heart was thumping in his chest like some lovesick schoolboy's as he braced himself. The light at the window went out. Now or never. He couldn't wait. He dodged across to the back of the hotel, hoisted himself up onto a flat roof, worked his way around on the top of the veranda, trying to muffle the sound of his boots. He leaped up to reach her open window. Hauling himself up to wriggle over the sill, his spurs got tangled up in the curtains, and he clattered to the floor with a thump. A sharp scream split the darkness and Katherine cried, 'Who's there?'

'Sssh,' Pete hissed. 'It's me.'

Katherine fumbled to light the candle by her bed, raised it, and peered at him, her eyes startled. 'You!'

'Jest making a social call,' Pete grinned, getting to his feet. 'Wanted to thank you personal-like for saving my neck.'

'Keep away from me. I'll scream. You can't –'

Pete advanced towards her as she sat up in bed and backed up against the wall. He pushed in tight up against her, feeling her warm body naked under the gauzy material, embraced her and pressed his lips hard against hers. Katherine struggled to break free, to push him away, and as the kiss ended, she sat there, her scarlet lips partly opened, her green eyes luminous in the flame, staring at him, breathing hard, her fingers outstretched, quivering like tentacles that wanted to push him away ... or get hold of him again.

'That was a getaway closer kinda kiss, weren't it?'

'You, you insolent, disgusting –' She raised her right hand ready to slap him, but there was a clomping of bootsteps on the stairs and in the corridor and a thundering knock on the door.

'Katherine! Are you all right?'

Pete backed away behind the wardrobe, his hand going to his gun. Katherine frowned at him, swung out of bed and went to the door. She pulled her negligee together, and straightened her hair, before opening. 'What's the matter, John?'

'I heard a crashing sound and a scream.'

He half-stepped inside but she blocked his way. 'It's nothing. I was opening the curtains for some air and tripped over a table in the dark.'

'Is that all?' Chiltern glanced around the room, frowning darkly.

'I really must get some sleep. I'm exhausted. Goodnight dear.' She gave him a gentle peck on the cheek, and guided him out. 'I'm so thirsty. I'm going to ring for the girl to bring me some tea.'

'Right.' Chiltern cleared his throat, testily. 'Goodnight, Katherine.'

They heard his bootfalls recede along the corridor to his own bedroom, the door slam.

Pete's long fingers closed around her breast, his wounded hand sliding around her waist as she tugged at the bell rope. She giggled, unrestrainedly, as she fell on top of him onto the bed.

'You bastard,' she whispered. 'I've been in torment waiting for you.' She slid down him until she was kneeling on the floor. 'Let me get your boots off. Or do you like doing it with them on?'

There was a discreet tap at the door. Katherine

touched her lips and went to it. Opened it a crack. 'You rang, miss?' Katherine thrust twenty dollars into the girl's hand. 'Would you mind getting me one of those bottles of champagne we had for dinner? It helps me to sleep. Put it on the bill. The cash is for you.' She smiled at the girl, who peeped past her and saw a pair of spurred boots sticking out.

The girl gave an impish grin and said, 'Certainly, miss. I'll be back in two shakes. Or maybe three.'

TWENTY-ONE

' "Never trust anyone with all your love or all your money", a Mexican friend of mine used to say.'

'Don't patronize me, Pete Bowen. You and your cynical remarks. I know what you bin doin' all night.'

Pete shrugged with a grin at her father as they sat eating breakfast. 'I jest wanna be a uncle to the gal, not a patron.'

'Aw, don't take no account. She jest got a girlish crush on ya. You would a bin cynical if you had taken advantage of the gal's feelin's, thet's fer sure. I trust you, Pete. You're a friend. You hear thet, Judy? Mistuh Bowen's a friend of ourn an' that's all.'

Judy raised her eyebrows, as if to say, 'Men!'

'C'mon, gal. Let's gargle some more of that cawfee 'fore we start the chores.'

'Thanks!' Pete said, as she tipped the scalding brew over his pants. 'You damn lil bobcat.'

'Oh, sorry, Mistuh Bowen. Wouldn't like to damage your prospects.'

As he was riding along by the side of Lost Lake the next morning Pete heard a blood-chilling yell and saw an Indian come riding fast out of the pine woods. The stallion reared as Pete spun round to face the challenge.

He yanked his Winchester out of the boot, pulled it right-handed to his shoulder, jerking down the loading arm with his left-thumb, and aiming along the sights.

This was supposed to be the territory of the civilized tribes, and he hadn't heard of any hostile activity in the area, but maybe this feller had a bee in his war bonnet about the railway. He was coming charging on in a straight line, yelping and screaming, as if he'd got his fate trance on. He didn't even have a skull-cracker in his hand. Maybe he thought it was a good day to die?

Pete's inborn reaction was to begin to squeeze the trigger. He had been attacked by plenty of Indians in his time. The ornery illogical coyotes. You never could tell what they were playing at. But, wasn't there something familiar about that high-crowned hat with the feather in it, the shape of the young brave? It couldn't be?

It was! As the Indian reached him on his scrubby pony, and swirled around him in a cloud of dust, Pete scrambled from his saddle. The Indian jumped down. Pete gripped him in a bear-hug and swung him round, whooping his rebel yell (that had made many a blue-belly mess his pants).

'You young varmint you! I thought you'd gone to the happy hunting ground.'

'No,' Henry said. 'I'm not a ghost.' They sat down on a log, out of breath. 'What makes you say that?'

'Damn bounty hunter came ridin' in, said he'd got your head and wanted mine.'

Henry cracked out laughing and slapped Pete's shoulder. 'What did he get?'

'My finger!' Pete roared, and showed him. 'Cain't give nobody the sign no more.'

Any onlooker, of which there were none, would have found this noisy reunion a most improbable sight. Indian lovers were few and far between in those parts.

'That must have been the head of that thievin' Pawnee that crept up on me as I lay on the mountain-side with my injured leg. He stole the black stallion there. I kept him at bay with my carbine, otherwise he would probably have killed me and taken the booty.'

Pete decided they should celebrate with a mug of tea, so he quickly had a small fire going and his billy can on, as he filled the Wichita in on what had been happening. Howling Wolf pulled out his long stone pipe and lit up, and they passed it to each other and smoked.

'Yep. That Indian Killer must have thought that thievin' Pawnee was you. Still, Henry, that lets you off the hook. Everybody thinks one train robber's been accounted for.'

'Maybe the gods are on my side after all.'

'How's the leg, Henry?'

'Almost as stiff as my middle one.' Howling Wolf slapped his belly and guffawed. 'One thing's for sure. I can't sit cross-legged any more. Tell me, you sneakin' dog, what did you do with that woman?'

'Not what you're thinkin', Henry. I handed her back in prime condition.'

'You horny old rattlesnake. I don't believe you. And what did you do with my thousand dollars?'

'Is that enough sugar in your tea, Henry?' Pete asked, solicitously, passing the wooden mug across. 'Now this is somethun else you ain't gonna believe, but I give the whole two thousand away to a darling lil fair-headed chickadee.'

The Wichita hobbled to his feet with a howl of disgust. 'Hold on, hold on,' Pete beckoned him back down. 'Let me tell ya the whole story.'

The Indian youth mumbled something about whiteman speaking with forked tongue, but consented to listen, and, at the end, Pete said, 'So, you see, young feller, you've got part share in a fine little smallholding. Believe me, I've invested your money wisely.'

'Huh!' Howling Wolf said. 'A fine story. I expect you lost it all at the poker table. You're a born loser.'

'No need to get personal, Henry. It's the truth I tell ya. One day mebbe you'll meet Mr Vine and Judy. She's the sweetest blue-eyed babe I ever did see.'

'Knowing you, I expect you ruined her.'

'Henry, what a thing to say. To tell you the truth it was me who was fightin' for my virtue like an ole maid. That gal was mighty keen on the idee. I had to give her a lecture about chastity.'

Howling Wolf thumped his fist on his knee. 'You whites, you are crazy. Here's me desperate for a squaw.'

'The best things come to those who wait, Henry. Must say I was tempted and I envy the young buck who does rope that gal. Waal, we cain't sit here natterin' all day. I gotta be headin' on.'

He jumped up and started kicking out the fire. 'Where you going?' Howling Wolf asked.

Black Pete shrugged, scratched his beard. 'I dunno. I got an appointment to meet somebody. It's personal-like. A lady.'

'A lady? You damn randy bastard. What lady?'

'Nobody you know, Henry. Look, I reckon it's best not to let 'em know we're pals, or else they might start putting two and two together.'

'If you think I'm going to go on hiding out in the woods you're mistaken. I bin too damn scared to go in to Connor's Crossing lest they had a necktie party waiting. But I'm damn sick of living out in the wilds like some durn savage. I fancy a porterhouse steak smothered in onions, a pint of whiskey and a game of the holy poker. And a proper bed to sleep in.'

'Ain't your hunting skills improved any, Henry?'

'All I had for breakfast was a durn squirrel. Just a scrap of bone and skin, poor critter.'

'C'mon. Robinson's Landing ain't far. Watch out for that cheatin' son-of-a-gun of a trader and so-called banker. I've already had a run-in with him. But if you got money he'll put a feed into you.'

'I've got cash and I've got all those gold watches and jewellery from the robbery.' He patted a bulging sack. 'I ain't had the chance to spend anything.'

'I'll call in on my way back tonight and see how you're making out. Keep your cards close to your chest.'

When they sighted the cabin, Pete headed up onto the high ground to circle around it.' *Adios, amigo,*' he shouted.

TWENTY-TWO

'As soon as we get this section of the railroad finished we will arrange the wedding. Then we will really have something to celebrate.'

John Chiltern was busy poring over plans and maps in his office. Katherine had looked in to see what he was doing. She was impatient to get away. It was already noon. She had hoped her fiancé would have been going back up the track to look at the rebuilding of the bridge. 'What are you doing today, John?'

'I've got all this paperwork to wade through. You're looking very beautiful. Are you going somewhere special?'

'No, I just thought I'd go for a ride along the river. It's such a lovely day.'

She was radiant, a starched blouse clasped at her long slim throat by a cameo brooch, a brown bowler hat on her pinned red hair, and she was wearing a long chestnut riding dress and high-heeled boots. She brought a lump to Chiltern's throat to see her.

'I wish I could come with you,' he sighed. 'I'll send one of the men along to look out for you.'

'No,' she protested. 'I want to be alone. I can't bear one of those creatures trailing after me.'

'It's dangerous. You're not in Kansas now. God knows

who's hanging about in those woods.'

God knows! Katherine thought, and smiled at the idea. 'I'll be fine. I've got a rifle in the boot.'

'Be careful. There are bears. Wolverine. Snakes. I'm not trying to frighten you, but it's not picnic country.'

'Don't be silly. I can look out for myself.'

'I think we should go back to my place in Philadelphia for the wedding. Let's make it a big society do. There won't be any gossip there.'

'Gossip?'

'About, you know. The abduction. It's not been very pleasant. I'll be glad when this line's finished. Those damned Vines are trying to hold me up. We can take an extended honeymoon. New York. Maybe even London, Paris, Rome.'

'Really?' The idea did excite her. And she felt suddenly ashamed. What was she doing sneaking away for an assignation with some backwoodsman? Why was she betraying John like this? Betraying her father? Betraying her true world? Her own future?

For moments she thought, dully, of going back to the hotel, divesting herself of the silly riding gear. She could occupy herself reading, collecting wild flowers, pressing them, improving her mind. But the need for excitement, to see him again, was too strong.

'Goodbye, then. I'll be back for supper. Don't worry about me, if … if I'm a little bit late.'

At least I'm not married, she thought. I'm not committing adultery. I'm just sowing my wild oats before I have to settle down and conform.

She was riding side-saddle on her gelding as she followed the river. She had gone about five miles and had seen no sign of any other person. That, surely, must be the bend in the river, the flat of sand he had spoken of. The only sound was of the flooded river rushing and murmuring by her side, the occasional eerie cry of some bird, or creature, in the woods. She was too obsessed by the prospect of seeing him to pay anything much heed. Or to check if anyone was following her.

Those must be the two big rocks he had told her about, the narrow pathway between. The dark slit opened up before her. It was like entering a cave. Her horse refused, but she leaned forward, patted its neck, made a kissing sound with her lips, and the horse hurried through.

At first she thought that this cut-off bay of the river, with its crescent of shingled beach, was deserted. She heard a low whistle, and saw Pete sitting in the shade, his stallion tethered nearby. She shivered with a start of fear. There was always something so dark and menacing about him.

'Hi,' he said, in his quiet way. 'I thought you weren't coming.'

'I had difficulty getting away.'

Suddenly, Katherine wanted to go back. She felt ridiculous, in her fashionable dress, a girl who could get any man, coming here to meet this scruffy Confederate prairie rat. It was foolish. Utterly mad.

Pete got to his feet and grinned at her. 'Step down, your ladyship.'

Reluctantly, trembling as he reached out to touch her, Katherine did so. He pulled her into him, savagely, pressed her up against the flat cliff wall. His tobacco-scented hairy mouth was upon hers, as if desperate to devour her. One of his hands was fumbling to unbutton her blouse as his other caressed her hair.

Katherine gasped, and broke away. 'You don't waste much time, do you?'

'I'm hungry,' he said. 'I been waitin' too long.'

'Oh, my God,' she cried, and hung onto his strong shoulders and let him have his way, let him feverishly undress her.

They did not notice, carried away as they were, young Davey McPherson, who had climbed to the top of the cliff. He was almost tumbling over in his eagerness not to miss anything, his eyes protruding and his prominent nose twitching as he watched. 'Geesis!' he whispered to himself.

TWENTY-THREE

Howling Wolf was losing. Heavily. His poker was getting even worse than Pete's. Maybe it was the whiskey. It had mussed his mind and made him act the fool. Why was it Indians couldn't handle liquor? Something to do with their physical insides? Or mental balance? Was it that they just overdid it, seeking some vision, and went crazy instead? He hadn't gone crazy yet. But he was feeling that way.

He had found Jim Robinson alone in his log cabin store at Robinson's Landing, had filled up his belly with beaver tail stew and barley sugar, and invited the big storekeeper to play a hand. Robinson had given his snarling, bearded grin, and passed the jug of corn liquor as the game began. Howling Wolf should have seen it was only a ruse. White men weren't legally allowed to ply Indians with whiskey. It was unlikely Jim was doing it from the kindness of his heart. Pretty soon all Howling Wolf's cash had gone. He was sure Robinson was dealing off the bottom of the pack, but he couldn't see how. The gold watches, diamond pins and jewellery quickly followed suit. Robinson's big hairy hands raked them in across the table. Desperate, Howling Wolf bet his pony. That too went. So, it was stolen stuff, but he had no particular wish to lose it all.

'Aincha got anythun' else? How about them ear-danglers? What are they?'

'They amethysts.' Howling was having difficulty forming his words. 'No, you ain't havin' they. They got the magic. You can have they gun. You can have they knife. You can have they rattlesnake rattle. How' bout they hat?'

'Ain' much of a piece,' Robinson said, examining the ancient Navy Colt. 'OK. Sling it in the pool. Have another slug from the jug?'

Again an ace of diamonds appeared as if from nowhere, and Howling saw his revolver being raked in. Robinson snaked all the bits and bobs into the gunny sack, went over to his safe, unlocked it, slung the sack in, and slammed it shut.

'White man play with crooked hands,' Howling shouted, and gave a forlorn howl as he stood, and immediately tumbled backwards over a crate of beans.

'Watch what you're doin', you lousy stinkin' drunk Injin. Here, have your stupid rattle back. That's about all you're worth. Now git out of here 'fore I blow you to kingdom come with your own gun.'

At which, Robinson started blasting away with the revolver, making Howling Wolf dance back and forth as the slugs splattered into the floorboards. Drunk as he was, he knew better than to fight lead, and he jumped and toppled and crashed his way back out of the store.

'He is not a nice man,' he said to himself, as he lay on the ground. 'This is not my good day.'

'Get outa hyar,' Robinson shouted, coming out to throw a bowl of slops over the Indian. He got hold of the pony and led it to his stable. 'You lost this fair and square. So now vamoose back to where you come from.'

Howling Wolf staggered away, his hat tipped over his nose, heading for the woods. When he crashed into the undergrowth a tenth time he decided to stay there and sleep it off. Where, he wondered, had he left that durn carbine? That was all he had left.

Judy Vine had got tired of kicking her heels at home. Black Pete's behaviour had irritated her. How could a girl live forever in such a snake-infested backwater of a place with only a father for company? She harnessed the team and set off jingling along the trail down to Lost Lake. They were in need of flour, molasses, coffee, beans, sugar. Maybe Mr Robinson would give them credit now they had paid their debts.

'Hi!' she called, as she strolled into the store. 'What's that smell of gunsmoke? Who's bin havin' a party? Why are all these boxes knocked over?'

'Arr, some damn drunken redskin. He didn' like being beaten fair and square at cards. I had to throw him out.'

'Thought I heard some gunshots on the way here. Can I have me a nice lemonade, Mistuh Robinson? It's so hot.'

'Yeah,' he said, pouring her a mugful from a gourd suspended from a beam. He went to look out of the door. There was no sign of the Indian. No sign of anybody. Just the woods. And the lake shining, placid and blue. He returned and sat uncomfortably close to her. She could smell his rancorous sweat. 'A purty gal like you ought to be findin' herself a man, eh?'

'I ain' in no hurry.'

'How about thet tall gunman? Thought he was after you?'

'Who, him? No he's got an ole woman. He's gawn.'

'Gawn has he?'

'Yes,' Judy said, angrily downing the lemonade. 'Gawn to her.'

'Gawn, eh? Thet's good news.' Robinson assumed she meant the gunman had left the area. Now they would have no trouble getting the Vines off their land. He went and slammed shut the door. 'You help yourself to all the goods you want, Judy. All you gotta do is be nice to a man.'

'Hey,' she said, looking up, sharply. 'Don't shut the door. What you locking it for?'

'Shame to waste a nice warm afternoon,' Robinson said, lumbering back to her. 'You're gonna feel a lot nicer laying down on them sacks nekkid. Don't say you don't wanna.'

'No, I don't wanna,' Judy said, backing away from him, snatching up a broom. 'You stay away from me, you hear!'

Jim Robinson laughed, and growled, 'I had my eye on you for quite some while.'

The girl swung the broom at him, but he caught it, and pulled her to him, and she found herself pinned against the wall, his long brawny arms holding her, helpless, and he slobbered his tongue over her face. 'You gonna take that dress off nice and quiet, you gonna lie down and do just what I tell you, and you gonna tell nobody. You gonna come back and do it again tomorrer. It's the only way you and your old man gonna stay on your land.'

'I ain't gonna do nuthin',' she shouted. 'You leave me 'lone.'

'You don't want it easy way. Then take it hard.' He cuffed the girl across the face, knocking her head against the wall. He cuffed her again, and forced her down to the floor. Judy screamed, and battered at him with her fists. 'Go on, fight,' he said. 'I like it better that way.'

'You get off me, you hear,' Judy shouted, as he knelt

on top of her. Robinson cuffed her again and she began to sob. 'Leave me be. Please. Don't. No.'

'Please, eh?' Robinson chuckled, easily holding both her wrists in one hand. 'You begging me to? Is this what you want?'

'*No!*' Judy screamed.

A window of the store was crashed in. The muzzle of a Spencer carbine was poked through. Howling Wolf squinted through the cracked glass. 'I don't think she wants you to do that, white man. You better let her up.'

'You!' Robinson turned, his face livid with rage.

'You filthy Injin. I told you ...' He went for his revolver.

Howling Wolf's carbine crashed out lead, making a hole in the big man's chest. Robinson cupped the blood in his palm, studied it, shook his head foolishly and collapsed back on the girl.

'You OK, missy?' Howling smashed the rest of the glass in and climbed painfully through the window.

'Yes, I guess. Could you ... could you haul this brute offen me?'

'Sure.' Howling rolled Robinson over. He looked down at her as she lay there straightening her dress. The eyes as blue as California forget-me-nots beneath the mussed fair hair. 'You must be the lil chickadee.'

They stayed staring at each other for moments as if hypnotized. Judy felt as if the life was draining out of her, as if she were going to faint. She had never seen such a handsome copper-faced Indian youth before, even if he did smell of strong liquor, and seemed to have a stiff knee. He put a hand out and pulled her to her feet. She swayed, and he caught her in his arms. To him she seemed so young and frail. 'You sure you OK?'

'Yes, sure.' She smiled up at him. 'I jest felt groggy fer a moment, thassall. He klonked me. Hard. What did you mean, chickadee?'

'That's what Pete said. The purtiest lil thang he ever did see.'

'Pete? You a friend of his?'

'Sure am.'

'Don't tell me. You must be Henry. The strange one.'

'That's me.' Henry grinned widely. And squeezed the girl tighter in his arms. 'He's gone to visit a lady.'

'Yes, I know. It's OK, you can release me. I feel better now. What we going to do about *him*?'

'Scalp him,' Henry shouted, snatching up his knife from the table, stuffing his revolver back in his belt. He put a foot on Robinson's back and bent over.

'No!' the girl shrieked. 'They would know it was you.'

'Lucky for him I cain't bend my knee. Let's get outa here. I'm gonna get my pony and vamoose.'

'Not so fast,' a man's voice said. 'I'm holding you for murder, son. Don't you move.'

TWENTY-FOUR

Katherine rode back into Connor's Crossing as the sun was falling. She felt exhausted, sunburned, but fulfilled. It had been a wonderful afternoon. Even if one she must never repeat again. The depraved girls of the casino were sprawled on the steps of the building as she passed and they whistled and catcalled to her, as if they knew what she had been up to. She blushed crimson and trotted her horse into the livery. She and Pete had been lucky not to have been seen together. They were making their way back to the trail through the woods when they had heard riders. They had watched from cover and had seen her father and John and the big-jawed sheriff from Red Rock go clattering by. It looked like they were on their way over to Robinson's Landing. She could not think why. All she wanted now was to steam in a bath and change.

She was about to do this when there was a tap on her bedroom door. She imagined it was the boy with the buckets of hot water. She opened it to see Davey McPherson standing there, a rather foolish smile twisting his lips. 'Yes? What do you want?'

'A word in your ear, Miss Baxter. May I come in?' And he was pushing his way past her. 'I thought it best to get it over with while your father and Mr Chiltern are away.'

'What do you mean?'

He was an odd, rather sycophantic youth, with stooped shoulders, and a protuberant red nose. He had always seemed harmless before, one of her father's buffoons. Now he looked at her, and smiled, slyly. 'Well, we wouldn't want them to know about our little chat.'

'What on earth are you talking about, Davey?'

'Well, you know, this afternoon. Did you enjoy yourself? Well, you certainly looked as if you were.'

Katherine suddenly went very cold. 'What are you saying?'

'Do you want me to spell it out? Well, I thought, when you were up against the cliff wall it was very exciting. I thought at first he was doing it against your will. But when you went running down and stripped naked, and went larking and splashing about, and did it laid out on the rocks, that did not seem the case. A very good performance. I had a grandstand view. A pity I didn't have one of those new-fangled cameras.'

Katherine's legs seemed to give under her. She sat down on the bed. 'What is it you want?'

'Oh, I followed you back through the woods. Quite a tender leave-taking. You down on your knees. I thought you were praying to him. Didn't have a very good view that time. Of course, I realized you weren't.'

'You are really enjoying this, aren't you?' Katherine said. 'I can see your mouth slavering. How much do you want?'

'Well, you see my father never had anything. And your father's never been very nice to me. Davey do this. Davey do that. See this scar? He did that. I could tell you a few of the crooked things he's been up to. The people he's had killed. Why do you think your mother left? Well, a well-off young lady wouldn't miss, say, five thousand dollars.'

'Five thousand? Where do you think I can lay my hands on that?'

'I'm sure you could, if you tried. It would be a little gift for all my services. A once and final payment. I wouldn't come back. I could buy myself a little spread somewhere. Something like that.'

'You can go to hell,' she said, getting up, poking a finger at his chest. 'And get out of my room.'

'I'll give you a day or two to think it over. I wouldn't advise you to say anything to your bandit lover. If anything happens to me they would find all this written down and deposited at the bank.'

'Get out,' she shouted. 'I've had enough of your threats.'

But as the boy tottered in with the buckets of hot water to splash into her hip bath she remained seated on the bed, abstracted, mentally totting up how much cash she could raise. Her mind was in a panic. All she knew was she had to stop him.

TWENTY-FIVE

The sheriff of Red Rock had not wanted to travel the seventy miles to Connor's Crossing. It was way out of his usual territory. But, Baxter had beckoned (by means of the wire). And when Baxter beckoned you got yourself in motion. He was all for the quiet life. Six men had already gotten killed, and he had no wish to be the seventh. Baxter had a bug in his pants about some big, bearded saddle bum. Was he the man who took the train from Red Rock? Miss Katherine said he wasn't. So did Davey. So why couldn't they take their word for it? The sheriff had only met him once, the lanky stranger with the guns, and the challenge in his dark, burning eyes that fair made your throat go dry. If it was the man, and The Indian Killer hadn't taken him, he seemed to live under a lucky star. The sheriff had no wish to test that luck, or his shooting, further. But, he guessed justice had to be seen to be in motion, so he had picked up his guns, boarded the locomotive, crossed the plains with their rotting bison carcases, fallen asleep to the rhythm of the rails as they climbed up into the mountains of Indian Territory, climbed across the broken bridge in the darkness, and arrived at Connor's Crossing the next afternoon.

'There's something fishy about that feller,' Baxter told

him over a meal of fried chicken at the hotel. The nattily-dressed John Chiltern put in, 'I was in half a mind to hang him, but Katherine said "No". She, surely, would know him.'

(At that moment in time, along by the river, she had been in the middle of knowing him very well indeed.)

So they had mounted horses and ridden out to Robinson's Landing to look for him. As they approached the store on the lake they had heard an explosion, like a carbine, and found an Indian with a gun in his hand and Jim Robinson dead on the floor.

'Look at my dress, look at these bruises, I've told you half a dozen times he got me on the floor, he was trying to do horrible things to me. If this Indian boy hadn't happened along, hadn't heard my screams, I'd probably be dead now.'

The girl certainly looked upset. A young white girl who lived with her father up in the woods. If anybody had touched his daughter, the sheriff thought, he would have done the same. John Chiltern was all for charging her and the Indian with homicide. 'She's the Vine girl,' he said. 'They're nester scum.' The sheriff wasn't so sure. 'She don't seem the kinda gal 'ud lie over a thang like that.' It seemed a cut and dried encounter to him. The feller had got his deserts. The young Indian was to be congratulated, if anything. (And who wanted all the trouble of a court case?)

'Let's take a look in his safe, see what he's got,' Baxter said, a mite worried about any deeds of land Robinson might have been holding. And he opened it up.

'Take a look at this,' the sheriff said, opening a sack. 'Don't these look kinda familiar to you, Mr Baxter? Don't these things tally with what they said was stolen from folk on that train?'

'I do believe, yes, this is Katherine's diamond

necklace. I gave it her, myself. And this her pearl-encrusted reticule, and –'

'Say,' said the sheriff. 'Whadaya know? This hyar's Mr Mirick's gold watch. "For services to the railway", it says here. This is some find.'

'Is he the man you told to get out of town, Sheriff?' Baxter asked.

The sheriff rubbed his slack jaw, surveyed Jim Robinson laying on the floor. 'I do believe it is. Same build, same beard. His eyes were real fierce, but they gone kinda funny now. Yeah, that's him sure 'nough. Who'd a thought it?'

Baxter eyed John Chiltern and said, 'You're certain?'

'Sure I'm certain. Waal, that wraps the case up far as I can see. Both train robbers dead. Folks git their goods back. I'll be heading home tomorrow.'

'Son,' he said, turning to Howling Wolf. 'There's 500 dollars reeward coming your way from the railroad company. Mebbe this gen'l'man here will settle up with ya?'

Howling Wolf grinned. 'Must be my lucky day, after all. You white men aren't as bad as you are painted.'

'I wouldn't have believed it of Jim Robinson,' Chiltern mused. 'How could he have been in two places at once?'

'Musta gone to Red Rock while you were away,' the Sheriff said. 'This evidence don't lie.'

'I suppose not,' Chiltern said. 'But it's only 250 dollars for one man. The other feller got the Indian.'

'Oh,' Howling grinned. 'I'm glad we got both those bad hombres.'

Grudgingly, John Chiltern took a wallet out, placed 250 dollars in notes in Howling's hands. 'Here,' he said. 'Saves the formalities. Sign me a receipt. What's your name? You can read, can't you? If not, put your sign.'

'Oh, yes, I been to college out east. I've just returned

home. Henry Littlejohn's the name. I'm working on an alphabet of the Cherokee and Wichita languages. Very similar to yours. We don't make so much use of the letters b,f,l,m,p,q,x,y, as you. We like very much h and k. In a way, our language is less barbarous than yours.'

The two well-dressed white men looked as bemused as the sheriff by this information and watched Howling Wolf sign his name with a flourish.

'Me and this young lady are going to be married in a day or two, just as soon as we can find a preacher.'

'We are?' Judy echoed.

'Really?' the sheriff said. 'Waal, congratulations, son, and thanks for your help.'

'I'll send an undertaker out to take care of the corpse,' John Chiltern said. 'I do believe he conducts weddings as well.'

'So long,' Howling Wolf called, as the three men rode away.

They helped themselves to stores, loaded the wagon, hitched the pony behind, and headed back to the farm. The sun was setting over the lake, a colony of cormorants diving greedily for their supper, and migrating birds flying overhead. They heard a low whistle and Black Pete came riding out of the woods. 'What was that all about?'

'Yeeee-hooooo!' Howling cried, putting his arm around the girl, 'I've got myself a squaw at last.'

'I told you Henry, your day would come.'

TWENTY-SIX

Katherine didn't wait long. An extreme agitation had gripped her. A determination to do what a threatened woman had to do. After batheing, she dressed in her riding clothes, again. She moved like an automaton, as if her mind was on another plane. She saw Davey sitting on the steps of the log cabin casino. She beckoned him over, as if she had an errand for him.

'Meet me along the river where the trees begin. In twenty minutes. I will give you what you need.'

He smiled at her in his silly way. 'I knew you'd see sense, Miss Katherine. You got it all?'

'Yes.' It was getting dusk as she saddled her gelding once more and rode out to wait for him.

Katherine was sat side-saddle, a bag on her lap, when Davey arrived.

'Hi,' he said. 'This is real nice of you.'

'Good,' she said, and her voice sounded far away to her. She pulled a derringer five-shot from her velvet bag, aimed at close range. 'I'm going to give you what you asked for, Davey.' She fired three times, twice into his heart and once into his side as he tried to escape. She did not miss this time. Alarmed, Davey's horse galloped off back towards Connor's Crossing, and, as the boy slowly toppled off, his foot caught in the stirrup; he was dragged bumping along in the dust.

Katherine stared at the river for a long time before walking her horse back to the settlement.

TWENTY-SEVEN

Howling Wolf couldn't believe his luck. A kind of elation had filled his soul since rescuing the girl, since realizing that she loved him. He was too excited to sleep and rose before dawn, climbing high into the hills above the Vines' homestead. In a grove of sugar pines he suddenly saw movement. He froze and raised his carbine. Probably just a jack rabbit. No, it was big. It was a half-grown bear, snuffling through the brambles, and heading towards him. It paused and raised its snout. Had it scented him? He had never seen one so close before. Now it was looking straight into his eyes, and it was coming at him in a charge, its teeth bared. Howling Wolf stood his ground and fired. The bear kept on coming. He pulled back the hammer, ejecting the empty case, and fired. Again. And again. The crash of the carbine echoed barrelling through the canyon, three times. The bear slithered into him, knocking him aside, gave a roar of agony and died. Howling Wolf stuck his knife into its throat to make sure. But the .52 calibre bullets had found their mark. Howling Wolf leaped onto a rock, cupped his hands to his mouth and cried out his triumph in a long high-pitched wail. It was a Paean of victory to the Great Spirit.

'Maybe there's something in this Indian magic, after

all,' he mused. 'I am a true hunter now.'

The animal was a warm, furry dead weight, but he managed to heft it onto his shoulders and go staggering back down the hillside under it.

The shots and the howling had brought Judy, Mr Vine and Pete out. 'This boy sure is some feller,' Mr Vine said. 'I'm gonna be proud to have him as a son-in-law.'

'Waal, it sure is an improvement on chuckawallah lizard,' Pete drawled. 'Looks like bear steaks for breakfast.'

'Now I have to catch an eagle to make a war bonnet,' Howling Wolf said, as they hoisted the bear up on one of the lodgepoles and began to ease its coat off. 'What I will do is dig a trench over there, cover it with branches and leave pieces of bear meat on top to entice the eagle down. Then I will leap out of the hole to catch it with my bare hands.'

'I told you he was crazy, Judy, didn't I?'

'The poor ole bear,' Judy said. 'He looks kinda pitiful without his lovely coat, all pink and nude.'

'We can have the coat for a bed cover in our new cabin,' Howling said. 'I will start on my eagle trap after breakfast.'

TWENTY-EIGHT

'I gotta take Katherine back to Red Rock for trial,' the sheriff mumbled, apologetically. 'There's no way I can ignore it, Mr Baxter, it's more than my badge is worth. It's so obvious she done it, and she ain't denying it none.'

Mr Baxter nodded, gloomily, and John Chiltern asked to see her alone. The sheriff had locked his prisoner in her hotel room, so he opened up and let Chiltern in.

Katherine was in a stubborn, non-communicative mood at first, the cold mood that always oppressed him. But her eyes glittered as she burst out: 'I had to do it, John. He threatened to tell you things about me.'

'What do you mean?'

'About me and that man, Pete. I couldn't let him go around saying things like that. It was all lies.'

Chiltern considered her in silence for seconds. And struck her a backhander across her jaw. A trickle of blood came from her lip. 'They weren't lies, were they? It's you who's been lying all the time. You and this horse dealer. You disgust me. You whore.'

Katherine faced him, defiantly. 'I suppose it was you who sent Davey to spy on me?'

'You suppose right. Now I'm going to kill this man. He has caused enough trouble.'

'Don't, John, you can't. Pete will kill you.'

'He won't have the chance,' Chiltern said. 'He's going to get a surprise.'

He slammed out of the room without a backward glance. Baxter caught hold of his shoulder in the corridor, 'What's going on?'

'You go back to Red Rock with her. I'm taking my best men. The Vines won't stand in our way any more.'

When he had gone, Baxter went into his daughter. 'You've really made a mess of things, haven't you, girl? You've got the wildness of your mother.'

'I know now why she left,' Katherine said. 'If it hadn't been for all that depravity in Red Rock, hounding people off their land, even killing them. I must have known you were behind it. All that greed. If you hadn't brought those bully boys into the town that Indian girl wouldn't have been raped and murdered. None of this would have happened.'

Baxter shook his head, sadly. 'I suppose you're right. I'm going to get you the best lawyer I can, Katherine.'

TWENTY-NINE

John Chiltern found four of his railroad guards who could fight. They mounted up and galloped out of Connor's Crossing in a cloud of dust. They passed Robinson's Landing and rode on along by the lake. When they got near to Lodgepole Creek they pulled their lathered horses off the road, tethered them, and climbed on foot up around the back of the farm.

It was deathly quiet and they could hear only the faint sound of voices, people sat out on the terrace beneath the tumbledown thatch of the farm shack. Chiltern fixed some charges in cracks in the rock directly above them.

'There's going to be an unfortunate accident,' he whispered, the sweat dripping from his forehead, dampening the band of his hat. His hand was unsteady as he lit the fuses. He knew it was a momentous decision, knew he was doing wrong, but his anger and bitterness impelled him onwards. As the fuses fizzed the men dodged for cover.

'Watch out!' Pete shouted, as he saw a movement on the hillside. Judy and her father had gone inside to the kitchen. All he could do was roll down the hill for the cover of a rock as the explosion of the dynamite roared, reverberating through the valley, and huge slabs of rock slid and tumbled down to crush the Vines' home.

Black Pete ducked his head as rocks pelted down like bolts from the gods upon him, and a heavier boulder struck him on the shoulder, crushing his ribs and knocking the breath from him. As the dust cleared he heard yells from the men who were coming leaping down the hillside. He freed himself from the rubble, and managed to pull one of his Smith and Wesson's. They were almost by the buried farmhouse when he fired, crashing out two shots to send one of the men toppling to his knees.

Pete tried to climb to his feet, ready for any more of the men to appear out of the billowing dust. A bullet sliced his neck and he spun round to see another man jump out from the other side of the farmhouse. He aimed at his belt buckle and sent him spinning to hell.

'That's your last shot!' Chiltern's voice rang out behind him. 'Hold it right there. Throw that gun down. I'm gonna kill you. Turn round, slowly. I prefer not to shoot you in the back.'

'Why not make this between you and me, Chiltern?'

'Throw it down. Quick.'

Pete tossed his revolver away, and reluctantly turned to face his executioner. Ah well, he thought, I knew it had got to come some day.

'This is for Katherine, for ruining my woman,' Chiltern raised his rifle to aim pointblank at Pete's chest.

Howling Wolf raised himself from his eagle trap trench, pushing the camouflage of branches away, and threw a tomahawk unerringly, to embed in Chiltern's back.

'And that is for the people inside that house,' he howled.

'Oh, my God!' Chiltern cried, as he collapsed, sharp metal in his back, a stickiness of blood oozing into his coat. He wriggled like a landed fish, making futile efforts to claw at the hilt.

'You sure took long enough to make your move, Henry.'

'Ah,' Howling Wolf said. 'Wichita very patient.'

Pete dived and picked up Chiltern's rifle, rolling for cover as he heard a slither of scree and a bullet whanged chiselling fragments of rock into his face. He poked his hat up on the rifle barrel and it was blown flying away by another whistling shot.

'Ain't no point you men fighting,' he shouted up in a pause in the shooting. 'John Chiltern's outa action. You ain't likely to be gittin' paid. There's a gal and her Pa trapped in this rubble, or dead. You better come down and help us dig 'em out.'

The answer was another fusillade from the rocks. Pete watched the puffs of black smoke and squinted along the rifle sights at a crack between two boulders where the firing was coming from. He squeezed the trigger.

Up in the rocks a man slumped back; a blunt-nosed leaden 'man-stopper' lodged up his nose. 'Reckern there's one varmint left,' Pete hissed at the kneeling Wichita. 'Go git him, Henry. I'll cover ya.'

Howling Wolf put his knife between his teeth and began to dodge up the ascent, but a fourth man yelled, 'Don't shoot. I'm coming down.' He threw a revolver out and slithered down.'

Pete covered him for moments, put the rifle aside, and muttered, 'You better come put a shoulder to these rocks.'

'It weren't my idea,' the man whined. 'It was Mistuh Chiltern's.'

'You ready to swear to that?'

'Sure,' the man said.

'Git a hand to this timber.'

The gunman hesitated, but did as he was bid.

'God help them,' Howling Wolf said, as they tried to get into the shattered farmhouse. They heard a groan and a girl's whimper and they fought harder to get the struts and rocks shifted. Eventually they got to them. Mr Vine looked like a ghost, smothered in dust, and blood-streaked. His leg was twisted and broken. When they heard the explosion they had dived for the cover of the overhang against which the shack was built. Mr Vine's body had covered Judy and she was bruised and dusty but unhurt. She wiped a sprig of hair out of her eyes and whistled, 'Jiminy! I thought we were goners for good when all that stuff came raining down.'

'Looks like your hero here, Henry, saved the day. Him and his eagle catchin'!'

'You're bleeding, Pete.'

'Yeah.' A bullet had sliced a weal across his neck. He tied his bandanna tight around it. 'Guess these fellas oughta do more target practice. And if Chiltern hadn't liked the feel of his revenge I'd a bin gone by now.'

Outside they found the three men dead, but Chiltern was still breathing. Pete pulled the tomahawk out of his back. 'Guess we'd better patch the coyote up and send him back.'

'Won't he cause trouble?'

'Let him try.'

They fixed up Mr Vine's leg in splints and made him reasonably comfortable. Judy bandaged Chiltern, and with a coffee inside him he seemed to come round a little. They hoisted the dead men onto the wagon and laid Chiltern among them.

Pete was harnessing up the team when Howling Wolf came bounding as fast as his stiff leg would allow, down the hillside. He had been nosing around where the explosives had cracked away the cliff. He had chunks of black rock in his hands.

'Look at this!' he shouted.

'That's coal, you son of a gun.'

'There's a whole seam of it four feet thick.'

'Hey,' Pete called to the Vines. 'Looks like you won't need to scratch the dirt no more. You could be wealthy pit owners. If you let the railroad come through here this mine will be in an ideal situation. You can transport coal for sale to the north-east. And you can supply it to the railroad for fuel for their engines instead of wood.'

'Yipeeee!' Judy yelled, and hugged the Indian youth. 'We can afford to git married now.'

'I'm not marryin' you for your money.'

'Don't be a durn fool,' Mr Vine said. 'You got a 1,000 dollar share in this land. So has Pete. It's legally yourn.'

'Yeah, you grab that gal 'fore somebody else does. You can have my share as a weddin' present. I ain't never been partial to digging down holes in the ground. Not since that cave-in in a mine in Colorado last winter I had to go down.'

'Whoooheee!' Judy cried. 'Looks like things are gonna turn out jest swell. Where's that new dress of mine? Hope it ain't gotten spiled in the landfall. We'll drive in an' git hitched pronto. You want to, doncha, Henry?'

A smile split Howling Wolf's bronzed flat countenance. He took Katherine's amethyst ear drops from his lobes and gave them to Judy. 'You're gonna look like the belle of the ball. We'll go to one of those bailies you were telling me about. You can teach me to dance white folk fashion. Sweetheart, we're gonna dance all darn night.'

'Yooheeee!' Judy grabbed him and kissed him on the lips. Then she whirled him round. 'I'm gonna teach ya right now. I cain't wait.'

'Swing him, gal,' Pete called. 'Dozey do and promenade. While you're in Connor's Crossing you'd better put in an official notice that you're forming a mining company.'

'Reckon we should?' Howling Wolf said, pausing in the dance.

'Yep. You being a Wichita you're legally entitled to mine this Indian Nations land, whereas a white man wouldn't be.'

'Whooeee!' Howling yelped. 'In that case we better get goin'. I'll have to bury the hatchet with Mr Chiltern and tell him the railroad can come through.'

'Thought you'd already buried one,' Pete grinned. 'In his back.'

Pete turned to the fourth gunman, who was standing around looking edgy. 'As for you, hombre, these people could charge you with attempted murder, but they ain't that sort. I suggest it wise for you to ride on in with us. Explain what occurred. Looks like your pals backed the wrong side.'

'Ain't you comin' in to act as best man, Pete?' Judy asked. 'Pa will be all right on his own for one night.'

'Sure I will,' Mr Vine said. 'Git that wagon rolling. Go 'long, you young folks, have yourselves a good time.'

And that they did.

'Everybody's invited to the marryin',' Pete shouted, amid riotous cheers from the Irish railroaders and their women and kids. 'Drinks is on me. Roll out that whiskey.'

That was after they had thrown the bodies of the gunmen out of the wagon and their prisoner had told his tale.

'Seein' as how Chiltern pays your wages there ain't much pint in us prosecutin' him for attempted murder,' Pete yelled. 'We gonna let bygones be bygones.'

There was as yet no church or mayor's office at

Connor's Crossing. So the undertaker presided at the wedding in Frenchie's casino. Judy walked in, looking as pretty as a picture, on Pete's arm. Howling Wolf had borrowed a frock coat and top hat for the occasion. And a couple of the 'fallen doves' got decked up as bridesmaids.

From outside came the appetizing scent of Howling Wolf's bear barbecueing on a spit, and they all flocked outside for a feast. The fiddler began playing, the drummer a 'banging, and someone was fluting on pan pipes. The casino girls were given a night off and everybody began dancing and singing, and whooping and drinking, like wild dervishes from Africee!

'I sure lost a good dancing partner,' Pete said, as he grabbed Judy away from her new husband and whirled her around. She looked flushed and elated, blue eyes sparkling like the lake surface, as they fandangoed in the crush.

'You'll find yourself someone, Pete,' she said.

'She's all yours, Henry.'

Howling Wolf didn't need no urging, and whisked his bride up and away to a room at the back of the cantina (because there weren't no room at the hotel). And, my, how those boards bounced all night!

It must be admitted Black Pete imbibed much too much of the Knock 'Em Dead. He didn't know where he was. He staggered out into the tall grass with some gal. He couldn't make out who she was in the dark. But she sure knew how to do things to a man. The twittering of the birdies woke him and he opened his eyes to see the old whore of about eighty in his arms. She had such a sweet contented smile on her toothless chops he didn't like to wake her up. 'Sure is a funny old world,' he mused, as he got to his feet and wrapped a blanket around her. 'I coulda sworn she was a young gal.'

THIRTY

The little foal was weak on her spindly legs, but she cantered after her mother from one end of the corral to the other. She was black like her father, but with three white socks and a white blaze. She stood behind her mother and watched inquisitively as the grey mare drank from a trough of water. Funny behaviour, she seemed to think – these grown-ups got. She preferred to nuzzle at her mother's milk and would do for some while.

Pete fondled the grey's mane. He had raised her from a foal herself, when he had had a ranch in Texas, taught her all the tricks a wise cowhorse ought to know. He had planned that she should be his son Jim's horse. But, it wasn't to be. When his ranch had been burned down by the Murchisons, he had taken the boy to San Antonio and put him on the stage to Kansas City to live with his aunt. Then he had killed Old Man Murchison, as he sat among his rich cronies at the Cattlemen's Club, and ridden out on the grey. He had never gone back.

'She's been with me a long time,' he said to Judy. 'But I guess I'll have to leave her here for a year or so. Mebbe I'll come back and reclaim her one day.'

They could see Howling Wolf and Mr Vine hobbling about on their stiff legs, digging into the coal seam,

153

bashing away with sledgehammers and picks on the hillside.

'Doncha wanna stay and share in what we make?.'

'No. I was never much of a one for digging holes.' He smiled at the girl. 'I hear tell Katherine's trial coming up. I'm gonna go take a look.'

Red Rock courthouse was jampacked for the trial. It was something of a social occasion with ladies in their best dresses and hats. It was not often a leading citizen's daughter was charged with murder. Everybody was fanning themselves because of the heat and hoping for some salacious titbits to emerge. Mr Baxter had engaged a fancy lawyer from St Louis who was forever jumping up and appealing on points of law so that very little was revealed. Katherine lied with cool composure, haughty and beautiful as ever in a dress of black silk that heightened her blue-veined pallor. Her red hair, piled loosely on top, glittered in the sunlight. It was a simple matter. She had been riding in the woods when Davey, her father's trusted employee, had appeared, made insulting and indelicate remarks and tried to drag her from her horse. She had panicked and shot him in self-defence.

Katherine stuck to her story throughout the prosecutor's questioning, the ones that her lawyer would allow him to get in. The audience was disappointed. The jury retired for only ten minutes and trooped back to find her not guilty, with a rider of 'justifiable homicide'.

John Chiltern had made a good recovery from his tomahawk wound and was ruddy-faced, cutting his usual dandified dash, as he pushed his way through the crowd, his arm around Katherine. Baxter took her other arm as they made their way down the courtroom steps.

A cub reporter from the Red Rock *Reveille* blocked

their passage. 'What are your plans now, Miss Baxter?'

'She is coming home with me to Philadelphia,' John Chiltern said, in his loud, cultured voice. 'We are to be married within the month.'

A buzz of surprise greeted this announcement and the reporter pressed on: 'What about your railroad? Weren't you having trouble buying land?'

'There was a little contretemps,' Chiltern said. 'That has been settled now. The Vines, or, should I say the Littlejohns, have agreed to us going through their valley. They don't need the farmland now. They are busy with other projects. They are going to supply us with coal. Our work is pressing ahead. We intend to roll all the way through Indian Territory until we reach Texas.'

'Let's hope we can all live in peace now,' Baxter added, as they moved away towards the railroad station. A locomotive was stood there, steaming and belching waiting to move out back towards more civilized parts.

A tall man in a torn macinaw, high heel boots, and a grey bullet-scorched hat, was stood in the shade, out of the glare of the sun. He leaned his back against the clapboard wall and watched them through narrow eyes as they passed. Katherine started when she saw him, hesitated a second, meeting his glance, and walked on past. She held her head erect and stared ahead.

Black Pete struck a match on his boot and lit a nickel cheroot. He watched Katherine and her party board the train, and spat out a gob of brown juice into the dust. He strolled over the black stallion at the hitching rail. 'Hey-ho, Jesus, ol' fren',' he said, climbing up into the saddle. 'Guess it's time to mosey on.'

He rode, straight-backed, at a lope out of the township towards the westering sun. He would head through Indian Territory and along the Canadian River across the prairies. He had always had a hankering to see New Mexico. Maybe Arizona Territory.

As he passed beneath the egg-shaped red rock, once sacred home of the Wichita tribe, the locomotive began its noisy locomotion along the curving track, puffing and blowing, its bell clanging mournfully, back towards Kansas City.

On the train Katherine saw the lone horseman and smiled to herself. How could she go with him? It had all been a foolish dream.

AFTERWORD

'Running a coal mine sure ain't easy.' That was Howling Wolf's complaint some months later. He had hoped to provide jobs and prosperity for Indians in the area, but they too, like Black Pete, could see little benefit in spending their days down a dark dirty hole in the ground. They preferred to be out in the sunshine and the woods. Mr Vine and Henry worked hard, got the contracts, made a pile of dollars, but had to import Italian and Pennsylvanian miners to do the skilled tunnelling work. And with them came labour troubles and more headaches. They sold out to a man called McAlester, who had wed an Indian girl. The coal mine eventually became one of the biggest in Oklahoma Territory. Mr Vine had a wonderful time wasting his share on a riverboat trip down the Mississippi; he lost the lot on the roulette wheel and died of a heart attack in a creole 'crib' in New Orleans. Howling Wolf followed his dream of founding a new town, Soda Springs, for Wichitas and Cherokees, and produced the first newspaper in the Cherokee language. Red Indians, unfortunately, had no great fondness for reading, preferring to recall past glories around the camp fire: circulation slumped and Henry gave up on the idea. He built a log cabin school to teach Indian children English and law so they would be well-prepared for the wily ways of the white men. This was not a lot of good to them. In later years, when the government let settlers swarm over their land in the great land rush, they were cheated hand over fist. So it goes! None the less, Mr and Mrs Littlejohn lived very happily and called their firstborn Pete, after a good friend of theirs (who they heard had been caught up on the frontier in the Apache Wars). And their second, a daughter, Moon on the Lake. And their third. ... he was my great-grand-daddy. That's howcome I know these things!